ONE OF
OUR OWN

ALSO BY LUCINDA BERRY

ONE OF OUR OWN

A Thriller

LUCINDA BERRY

EMILY BESTLER BOOKS

ATRIA

New York   Amsterdam/Antwerp   London
Toronto   Sydney/Melbourne   New Delhi

EMILY
BESTLER
BOOKS

ATRIA

An Imprint of Simon & Schuster, LLC
1230 Avenue of the Americas
New York, NY 10020

For more than 100 years, Simon & Schuster has championed authors and the stories they create. By respecting the copyright of an author's intellectual property, you enable Simon & Schuster and the author to continue publishing exceptional books for years to come. We thank you for supporting the author's copyright by purchasing an authorized edition of this book.

This book is a work of fiction. Any references to historical events, real people, or real places are used fictitiously. Other names, characters, places, and events are products of the author's imagination, and any resemblance to actual events or places or persons, living or dead, is entirely coincidental.

This Emily Bestler Books/Atria Paperback edition April 2025

EMILY BESTLER BOOKS/ATRIA PAPERBACK and colophon are trademarks of Simon & Schuster, LLC

Simon & Schuster strongly believes in freedom of expression and stands against censorship in all its forms. For more information, visit BooksBelong.com.

For information about special discounts for bulk purchases, please contact Simon & Schuster Special Sales at 1-866-506-1949 or business@simonandschuster.com.

The Simon & Schuster Speakers Bureau can bring authors to your live event. For more information or to book an event, contact the Simon & Schuster Speakers Bureau at 1-866-248-3049 or visit our website at www.simonspeakers.com.

Interior design by Jill Putorti

Manufactured in the United States of America

1 3 5 7 9 10 8 6 4 2

Library of Congress Cataloging-in-Publication Data

ISBN 978-1-6682-0962-2

My forever partner in crime, Molly

CHAPTER ONE

FELICIA: National Suicide Prevention Lifeline, this is Felicia.

CHLOE: [sobbing]

FELICIA: It's okay. I'm here. You're not alone. You're okay . . . can you tell me your name and where you're calling from?

CHLOE: [more crying, the sounds of a car driving past]

FELICIA: Hello? I'm hearing some traffic around you. . . . Are you safe? Can you tell me where you are? Are you in danger?

CHLOE: Please . . . help me . . .

FELICIA: Are you in danger?

CHLOE: I can't do this. I just can't do this anymore. I can't go to school tomorrow.

FELICIA: How come you can't go to school? What's going on there?

CHLOE: Oh my god. . . . There's a video. I can't believe there's a video. They recorded it. . . . I didn't know . . . I'm totally naked. [gulping breath] They're sending it around and now everyone's seen it. [breaks into sobs]

FELICIA: It sounds like you're in a lot of pain, and I want to help you. You don't have to go through this alone, okay? You're not alone. I've got you. But first, I just have to ask you some questions to make sure you're safe. Is that okay?

CHLOE: [deep breath] Yes.

FELICIA: Are you currently having thoughts about harming yourself, or not wanting to be alive?

CHLOE: [long pause] Yes.

FELICIA: Do you have a plan?

CHLOE: [softly] Yes . . .

FELICIA: Can you tell me about it?

CHLOE: My dad has a gun, and I know the combination to the safe. So that's how I got it, but I've never used a gun before. I don't know if I'll do it right. What if I do it wrong? What if I screw it up like I screw everything else up? . . . That's all I keep thinking about. Like, what if I do this, and it doesn't work? [talking speeds up] What if I blow half my face off and have to live that way? Or I paralyze myself somehow so I'm stuck, like, trapped inside my body and I can't try again? What if I don't die? I don't know how to shoot a gun. I—

FELICIA: Do you have the gun with you?

CHLOE: Yes.

FELICIA: And where are you right now?

CHLOE: I'm at the park.

FELICIA: A park? It's very late . . . are other people there with you?

CHLOE: I'm alone. It's just me, I think.

FELICIA: Can I ask why you're at the park?

CHLOE: Because I didn't want my parents to be the ones to find me. I couldn't do that to them. . . . It would destroy my mom.

FELICIA: That was thoughtful of you. It sounds like you really care about your parents. Have you tried to talk to them about how you're feeling?

CHLOE: Are you kidding me?! They'll want to know what happened and I can't tell them that. It's so humiliating. No way. I can't.

FELICIA: It's okay. It's okay. . . . Do you want to tell me what happened? Sometimes our callers find it helpful to talk about what's on their minds, especially if they can't talk about it with the people that are closest to them. I'm just here to listen, not to judge you. [pause] It sounds like the pain feels so intense that you're thinking of–

CHLOE: [angry] I'm not thinking about it. I'm going to do it. I'm just scared I'm not going to do it right.

FELICIA: Okay, I hear you, but I just want to point out you did call me before doing anything, so there must be a small part of you that doesn't want to do this, that wants to stay alive. . . . Don't you think? Can we try to talk to that part of you? [pause] I know it hurts a lot right now, and feels like there's no way out, but I really believe I can help you, if you let me.

CHLOE: You can't help me . . . nobody can.

FELICIA: Sweetie, I understand you don't see any hope right now, but I do. And not just because I'm trying to make you feel better. . . . I've been through a really dark period in my life, too. I know what it's like to feel hopeless and alone. [pause] But what if I told you that you wouldn't always feel this way? That this experience–whatever happened, whatever you went through–did not have to destroy you. What if you knew in three months, or a year, you'd feel better and whatever you're feeling right now would be gone?

CHLOE: That's not going to happen. I'm never going to feel better. Besides, even if I do feel better, everything's ruined. My life is over. You don't know what it's like at my school. Everyone at Buckley is so fake and phony. They all just talk about each other behind their backs. And now they'll never stop talking about me. They—

FELICIA: I'm sorry, did—did you say Buckley? Buckley Preparatory High School?

CHLOE: You know it? I thought this was, like, a random counselor or something.

FELICIA: Sure, I do. You know how you got that message in the beginning saying your call was being routed to the nearest center?

CHLOE: Mm-hmm.

FELICIA: 988 is a national hotline, and it's staffed by people at call centers around the country. When someone calls, the system logs them by their area code, and then sends them to their local area, so we can help them find resources close to them. Wouldn't do any good if I offered you a place to get counseling in Arizona if you live in New York.... So yes, I'm familiar with Buckley. But I'm also familiar with the other schools in the area. I just recognized the—

CHLOE: Oh my god, someone's coming. I've got to get out of here. They're coming!

FELICIA: Who is? Do you know them? Are you in danger? [pause] Please, just stay on the line. Can you stay on the line with me? Stay on the line with me. Just stay on the line . . .

CHLOE: [rustling, footsteps] I have to go. I have to go.

FELICIA: Please, let me help you! I can help you. Tell me where you are. I'll get you help . . . don't hang up.

CHLOE: [talking softly; breathing hard] I can't! I've got to go.

FELICIA: Listen, I want you to listen to me very carefully. Are you listening? Please put the safety on the gun. Do you know how to do that?

And then I want you to get to a safe place. Can you get to a safe place? That's all you have to do.

[pause]

FELICIA: Take down my number, okay? Can you do that? I'm giving you my cell, so you can contact me directly. Please just stop and put my number in your phone. It's 608-555-9982. Did you put it in your phone? Put it in your phone . . . 608-555-9982. Honey—honey, are you there? Are you safe? Please, just, just answer—

[line goes dead]

I jumped up from my desk and whipped around, searching for my supervisor, Phillip. He was already racing toward me with his headset wrapped around his shoulders. The cord dangled behind him. He must've yanked it right out of his computer.

"What in the hell were you thinking?" he screamed at me, waving his hands around. "You can't give a caller your personal phone number!"

"That's what you're worried about right now?!" I grabbed his arm and pointed at my computer monitor. "We have to get her back on the line! How do we get her back? Did you call 911? I thought you were supposed to be calling 911!" The moment she mentioned a gun, I messaged him that we had a potential caller in need of emergency services, and he jumped on the line, per our protocol. We were the 911 of mental health, but sometimes, in cases like this, we had to call the real deal.

He shook his head and shoved me aside. He leaned over my computer and frantically typed, pulling up the call data while he talked. "I didn't have her on the line long enough to track her." Unlike 911, we didn't have the capability to track people's locations when they called in. Complete anonymity was exactly why the call center worked.

"What are we going to do, Phillip? What are we going to do?" This had been my biggest fear since I started volunteering at the center two years ago—someone hurting themselves while they were on the line with me. And it's not like it hadn't happened. Sometimes people were in real physical danger by the time they called us. They'd already taken a bunch of pills, or were in the middle of hurting themselves. And this girl wasn't just a threat to herself—she was armed and it sounded like someone was chasing her, too. "Did you hear her say they were coming?"

He ignored me and continued working. Elaine rushed to join us and she stood next to me, putting her arm around my waist. We were the only ones working that night, since Sean had called in sick, and I was glad to have her by my side. We weren't just colleagues. She was one of my closest friends, too.

"I'm sorry," she said. She was actually the one that was supposed to take this call, but she'd been on a break so I'd grabbed it for her.

"It's okay," I replied as the data finally loaded in the queue. It's not like she'd passed off a difficult caller on purpose. We never had any idea what was coming.

The dialogue box opened on my screen. I quickly unplugged my headset so we could all hear it and turned up the volume on my speakers. The three of us barely breathed as we listened, straining for any clues to who the girl was, where she could be now, or other things I might've missed in the moment.

My knees went weak and my heart stilled in all the places it had when I first heard it, especially when she mentioned Buckley Preparatory School. It was just as shocking hearing it the second time, even though I knew it was coming. It just reinforced how close this one hit home—my son, Hunter, was a junior at the same high school.

CHAPTER TWO

I set my keys on the entryway table and crept into Hunter's bedroom without taking my shoes off. I had to see him. It was only six thirty a.m., so I had another half hour before he got up, but I couldn't wait.

My last call had shaken me to my core. The girl never called back. Each minute dragged while I waited for the switchboard to light up with a caller, or for my phone to ring, but neither did. Eventually, there was nothing else I could do except come home. Still, it felt wrong.

Phillip was livid I'd given her my personal cell phone number. It was the first rule of working at the center—do not give out your personal information. But what else was I supposed to do? I just reacted to this girl's desperation. It wasn't like kids never called in to the center: they did, all the time. But most of them were pranks. Sick jokes. They thought it was funny. More than once, I'd spent hours on a call with a teenager only to catch the sound of snickering in the background. Our training with teenagers was largely focused on deciphering the real calls from the fake ones early on so we didn't waste our time.

I've only had two other real cases from young callers, and I was just as bothered by them. It felt like the level of responsibility skyrocketed when you were dealing with a child, especially being a parent myself. It was impossible to help other people's children without thinking of your own, and if the roles were reversed, I'd want someone to do everything in their power to save my son.

It was my own family history that had brought me to the call center. My youngest sister died by suicide in college. She took her physics final and told her friends she'd meet them for lunch after she had a shower. Her roommate found her hanging in their closet an hour later. Our family was wrecked. Torn apart in ways we've never recovered from. You don't get over something like that. We'd moved on, but only because the world kept moving. Not because we wanted it to.

There were so many hard things about that time, but for me, the worst part was the fact I'd had no idea she was even struggling—nobody had—and I clung to the fantasy that I would've been able to stop her from dying if she'd told me how she was feeling. As the oldest of four girls, I'd helped her with everything from learning to walk to riding a bike and every milestone in between. That's what I did. I was her big sister. I could've helped her, and it didn't matter how many times people said it wasn't so—I still believed it was true, despite all the hours I'd spent in therapy. My therapist had been the one to suggest volunteering at the center. She said it might help heal that part of me. Maybe if I could help someone else, it'd lessen the pain over not having been able to help Holly. I'd balked at the idea at first because I had absolutely no training in mental health, but I'd been surprised to discover you didn't need any. Not any more than the thirty-hour crisis counselor training they provided for the volunteer staff. That said, none of their initial trainings or the follow-up ones I'd done had prepared me for what I'd just heard.

Hunter stirred and I looked down at him. He was curled up on his side. His stuffed animals from childhood surrounded him. He still slept with them every night, even though he was seventeen. They were tucked away in a drawer underneath his bed each morning and brought back out every night. They'd probably go with him to college. I loved this about him. My sweet boy.

I leaned over and sniffed the top of his head, careful not to wake him. I'd been watching him sleep ever since he was born, and sometimes, on nights like tonight, he looked like the baby he was back then. Dark lashes resting on his rounded cheeks. Puckered pink lips. Smooth, shiny face. And just so peaceful.

My heart ached for him, but not just him. All the kids growing up in this generation. That poor girl tonight was wrecked because of some stupid video going around. There were so many cautionary tales out there about this generation's social media use. Between knowing what their friends were doing any second of the day and a nude pic they'd sent to their crush, who didn't keep it a secret, there were land mines everywhere. I never would've survived middle school. I didn't know how they did it.

I wondered: Did Hunter know the girl that called tonight?

Did I?

It's always possible I'll get a call from someone I know, but most people didn't give any identifying information, and I'd never recognized anyone just by the sound of their voice. Elaine swore she recognized her dentist once, but nobody believed her. There was a strict protocol for transferring a call if there was a personal connection, and I'd gotten Phillip on the line partially for that reason, but it all spiraled so quickly.

Buckley was one of only two private high schools in our small Wisconsin town. There were just over three hundred kids in the entire school, so everybody knew everyone else, and if some awful video was circulating, she wasn't exaggerating when she said that everyone would see it. Including Hunter.

I quickly grabbed his phone from the nightstand next to his bed and typed in the code before I changed my mind. He'd be furious if he caught me going through it, but I wasn't interested in snooping into his personal life—I just wanted to find the video. If I could do that, then I could figure out who the caller was and let her parents know she was in trouble. I'd probably lose my job at the center, but at this point, I didn't care. This was too important.

I knew Hunter and his friends loved Snapchat, so I went there first, but nothing made me feel older than that app. It made no sense to me, even when he first got it and tried explaining things. That's probably why they all used it—because none of the adults understood how it worked. Then I remembered what Hunter had told me: everything deleted within twenty-four hours. I skimmed through his stuff, but from what I could tell, there was nothing there. Just countless goofy selfies and random pictures sent among him and his friends.

Next, I went through his recent texts, but they were mostly about homework and running. Hunter was captain of the cross-country team and an honor roll student, so his life was packed with practices, meets, and homework. Instagram proved pointless, too. He and his friends rarely posted anything. I wasn't sure why they even had it. They were starting to look at Instagram like my generation looked at Facebook—old and outdated. It sounded like they spent most of their time on Snapchat and Tik-Tok. His TikTok inbox was filled with stupid pranks and dance videos. There was nothing sinister.

I laid his phone back on the nightstand. He'd wake up with no notifications on his phone, and immediately suspect I'd been through it, but he was just going to have to deal with it. If he hadn't gotten the video, maybe it hadn't been shared as widely as the girl thought? Maybe it was never shared at all, and she was just getting carried away. Kids said all kinds of things.

Or maybe I was just too optimistic.

Where was she at this exact moment? Was she safe? What was she doing? I couldn't shake her. I mean, what if I knew her parents? It wasn't outside the realm of possibility that I had met this girl. Hunter had lots of female friends, and they moved in and out of the house along with all of his male friends. The only difference between them and the boys was that the girls weren't allowed to stay overnight. But this caller could've been in my living room. I might have ordered her pizza, asked her about her college plans or her prom dress.

My movement made Hunter stir again. He rolled over within seconds and slowly opened his eyes to look up at me.

"Mom? What's wrong?" he said sleepily, like he wasn't sure if he was awake or dreaming. Finding me sitting on his bed staring at him for no reason was definitely out of the ordinary.

I brushed the chestnut curls off his forehead. "Hi, honey. Sorry I woke you a few minutes early. Did you sleep well?"

He closed his eyes and murmured yes, rolling onto his stomach. I reached down and rubbed his shoulders like I used to when he was a baby. Actually, I'd rubbed his shoulders as he fell asleep until he was eleven years old, which was ridiculously old to keep it up, but he was my only child. I was never going to have another kid, so I held on to every stage for as long as possible.

I gave him a few more minutes before bombarding him with questions. "Sweetie, I want to ask you about something. Are you awake?" He grunted. He was probably afraid I was going to bring up his college essays again, since we were right in the thick of applications, and I'd been on him about them for weeks. "Is there any drama going on at school?"

"There's always drama at school, Mom. That's what you wanted to talk to me about at seven in the morning?" He laughed, pulling the covers around him.

"I was just wondering . . . if there'd been a video of a girl going around school?"

"A video of a girl? What do you mean?" His voice was muffled by his pillow.

"Just anything you can think of that got sent to a lot of people in the last couple of days." I couldn't have been more vague, but it was hard to ask him to help me find something when I didn't know what I was looking for.

"Like, someone had a video go viral?"

"No, I mean, something being sent around at your school."

"I can't think of anything, but that doesn't mean much. People are always sending stuff around. Was it a TikTok video? Which grade?"

"I don't know exactly what it was," I said, quickly realizing the futility of our conversation. I needed more information before I could ask sensible questions. "Can you just pay attention today? Let me know if you see anything out of the ordinary?"

He sat up and rubbed his eyes. "I guess. Why are you being so weird? What's going on?"

I pulled him close for a hug, squeezing him tight. I wanted to tuck him back inside my body, where I could keep him safe. "Oh nothing. It was just something someone referenced in the mom group chat. Don't worry about it." I held him close, breathing in the scent of him. So grateful he wasn't the girl on the phone. He was okay. Here. Alive. Safe. My heart swelled with love and gratitude.

CHAPTER THREE

My deposition was grueling. Nobody ever wanted to talk to family law attorneys, and my client's husband wasn't any different, but somebody had to help people get divorced, and I was determined to help these two do it with dignity. That's how I'd built my practice—Divorces with Dignity—over the last ten years, trying to keep an already painful process from getting ugly. Some days were harder than others. This was one of them.

I was halfway through my questions when my phone buzzed with a call. Normally, I tucked it away so I wasn't distracted or bothered by it, but I'd had my phone on me since leaving the call center, hoping the girl would reach out. I'd been obsessively checking it to make sure I hadn't missed anything, switching the volume on and off. I even had my assistant call me to see if it was working, as if it'd suddenly broken or something. It was irrational, but I was irrationally worried about her.

Had someone hurt her? Had she hurt herself? Could she be dead? My thoughts chased themselves in circles.

The opposing counsel was going on and on about the assets she believed her client's wife was hiding, but I couldn't pay attention to anything she was saying. All I wanted to do was answer my phone, but there was no way to do it, especially not with this attorney. She was as nasty and as high-maintenance as her client. The phone finally stopped vibrating against my thigh. I waited for the follow-up buzz, alerting me that I had a new voicemail, but there was none.

The next forty-five minutes were brutal. Each one dragged. As soon as we were done, I quickly thanked everyone and dashed out of the conference room. I whipped out my phone to see the call I'd missed. It was an unknown number. I broke out in a cold sweat.

Could it be her?

Calm down, I told myself, trying to steady my nerves. It was probably just a stupid sales call. But what if it was her, and she needed me? I hurried to my office and quickly shut the door behind me. I logged onto my computer and stared at the blank screen like I'd been doing all day, trying to figure out a way to find her. But it was impossible— the only detail I knew about her was that she went to Buckley. It was a small school, but even so, there were still over a hundred and fifty female students. I anxiously tapped my fingers on the desk, and then suddenly, a text alert. An unknown number again, but a different one than the missed call. My heart skittered against my chest.

It's me

I jumped up from my desk and let out a whoop, dancing around my office. She was alive! The tension in my neck released. I quickly texted before I lost her again.

The girl from last night? The one who called in?

I asked just to be one hundred percent certain.

Yep

Such a nonchalant, normal response. Good. Maybe she was feeling better.

I'm so glad you reached out. I've been so worried about you. Are you okay?

Idk

Are you safe?

Yes

Are you sure? It sounded like someone was chasing you at the park.

She inserted a laughing emoji. It was just some dog but it sounded like a person so I totally freaked out. Just my luck to get kidnapped by some weirdo when I'm trying to— This time she inserted the squirt gun emoji—myself. Another laughing emoji.

Oh, thank god. As long as she was safe and alive, there was still hope. I furtively glanced at my office door like someone might come in and know I was doing something wrong. I had to remind myself that all I was actually doing was texting. I stared at the phone. Now that I had her, what did I say? There weren't any protocols for this.

Are you at school?

I faked sick and stayed home

She inserted a sick emoji at the end. My head spun. Was it good she stayed home? Or would it call more attention to the situation? I had no idea.

How are you doing? Are you feeling any better?

I tiptoed around the things I wanted to ask; I didn't want to spook her. Empathetic and supportive. That's what I'd be. Just like I was at the call center.

She sent back a bunch of emojis with all kinds of different feelings. I had no idea what they meant or how to interpret them. Ever since Hunter informed me the sobbing your eyes out emoji was now used as a response for something funny, I'd given up trying to use them right. What was she trying to tell me? Why couldn't she use words?

That sounds like a lot, I responded, with a confused emoji of my own.

Lol, she wrote, followed by a roller coaster.

I'm so glad you reached out. I want to help. How can I help you?

I stared at the phone, reading and rereading what I'd sent. I sounded like a customer service agent. I wished she'd just call. She wasn't going to open up to me like this. But suddenly, the text bubbles danced on my screen. Dance and stop. Dance and stop. And then they just stopped. Whatever she'd written, she didn't hit send. She must've changed her mind. What was she going to say? I couldn't help her if she wouldn't talk. This was so different from the call center.

Are you still there? I couldn't wait any longer. I only had ten minutes before I had to be in court, and I had to do something.

I have a new plan.

What did that mean? A plan to end things, or to get help? This was why I hated texting. It was too ambiguous. It was hard enough to help them on the phone. This was almost impossible.

Did you call me earlier? Can you call me again?

I can't anymore

This time I was the one to do the three-dot dance for her as I typed and erased my response before finally settling on Can you tell me more about the plan? I just want to make sure you're safe.

I'm going to shoot them first

Nausea flooded my throat.

Who? I asked, like I didn't already know.

The boys who hurt me.

Do you think there's another way? Think about what happens if you do that.

I don't care. It doesn't matter, since I'm leaving anyway. I decided last night. They should have to pay for what they did to me. Why should I have to be the only one suffering? They're just going about their lives like it's no big deal. No way. And you know what else? I don't want people to remember me like that. Not on that video. I'll make a new video when I do it. I'll be the girl that got payback.

My blood froze. Countless images from school shootings flashed through me. Was that what she was planning? My head spun with possible scenarios, each one more terrifying than the last.

I understand you're in a lot of pain, and I know it feels like it will last forever, but it won't. Can we try to find a different plan together?

You wouldn't be saying that if you knew what they did to me

What did they do? Was I supposed to ask that? I didn't know, but I felt like I was gathering her statement, so it seemed important. The seconds dragged while I waited for her to respond.
Still nothing.
Was it too triggering? Maybe I shouldn't have asked. Then, finally:

Promise you won't tell anyone?

I promise. I knew I had to say it, so she'd trust me. In reality, I had no idea what I'd do next or who I was going to tell, but I was going to have to tell someone. Could the police trace unknown numbers?

They drugged me and took turns

She didn't have to clarify. I rubbed my hands on my face. A throbbing pain grew behind my eyes. It'd be a full-fledged migraine by tonight. I checked the time again: two minutes until trial.

How did I respond to that? I was a lawyer. Not a therapist or mental health professional of any kind. In the thirty hours of training to work at the call center, nothing had prepared me for anything like this. All I could think about was Phillip's anger about my having given her my number in the first place. This was why. Right here. I was so far out of my depth, and I had no time.

I'm sorry, I'm at work and have to be in a meeting very soon. Can we talk again later? Can you promise me that you won't do anything until we talk again? You won't hurt yourself or anyone else. Please?? I put a series of praying hands at the end.

A few excruciating beats passed.

I can't do it today anyway

Sweet relief flooded my veins. At least I had until the end of the day to figure something out. To come up with a plan.

Okay. Please, just wait until we talk. We'll figure this out together.

There's nothing you can do

Please let me try

Let's chat later xo

Xo? She ended the conversation with hugs and kisses? I didn't know what to say or do, so I just responded with a heart. I tucked my phone in my pocket and grabbed my briefcase.

What had I gotten myself into? And what was I going to do now?

CHAPTER FOUR

I hurried into Nickelsons to meet my friend Stan after work. We'd met in law school at Hamline, in one of my criminal justice classes. He was studying to be a police detective, and I was going for my juris doctorate. Years ago, we'd casually dated, but there hadn't been much of a spark. We were way better as friends, and we'd stayed connected all these years. We'd consulted on a few cases together. I knew I could trust him.

He was already at the bar and rose from his spot when he saw me. Tall and broad shouldered with matching brown hair and eyes, he looked a little like Miles Teller. He gave me a huge hug and pointed to the two beers in front of him. "Figured you needed this, stat."

I slid onto the barstool. "You wouldn't be wrong."

He'd been my first call on the way to court this afternoon. I couldn't go in knowing there was a girl out there potentially plotting to shoot a group of students and then turn the gun on herself. I'd filled him in on all the details about what had happened with the girl since last night. This was way bigger than me, and I needed his help.

"I talked to my supervisor and a couple of other officers about what's going on, and I'm sorry to tell you there's not much we can do at this point. There's no way to track the calls at the center, even if the request comes from law enforcement, because the actual geolocations aren't part of the software. They don't track or trace anything." I sighed, and he could sense my frustration. "Now, they do record them, so there's the potential to go back through the call and try to pick up any clues or ideas about who she is or where she might've been calling from. I'm not sure if there's anything there, but it's something. Do you have access to your previous calls?"

"Yes, they're all recorded." Even if Phillip hadn't been listening to the call, he still would've found out I'd given her my phone number after reviewing the tape.

"Have you listened to it? You might want to think about doing that. Just see if you hear anything you might've missed the first time."

I nodded. "We listened to it twice last night. The only thing that stood out was her mentioning Buckley. I just don't know what to do, Stan. What else can I do?"

He reached over and gave me a side hug, but I didn't want a hug. I wanted answers. A plan. I couldn't stand living with this ambiguity.

"Can I be totally honest with you?" I nodded, and he exhaled slowly. "I'm not convinced she's serious about her threats. For starters, you know as well as I do that most violent crimes are committed by men, especially when it comes to mass shootings. Rarely women. Second, she's a teenager, and I can't tell you how many threats the department gets that end up being pranks. These kids can have some sick and twisted forms of fun these days, especially if they're recording it for social media."

I shook my head at him. "I already told you—it wasn't a prank. Everyone at the call center agreed that it sounded extremely serious, even my supervisor, who's been there ten years."

Stan cocked his head to the side. "Really? I don't want to sound insensitive, but she's in a park with a gun in the middle of the night. And then she gets chased? It sounds like a poorly written horror flick."

"I agree. It sounds totally dramatic and over the top, but you didn't hear her voice. You can't fake that kind of raw emotion."

"Have you heard anything from her since?"

"Not since the texts before court. I was waiting to contact her until after we met. I wanted to get your take on everything." I pulled out my phone, unlocked it, and handed it to him. "See what you can do."

This was the real reason we were meeting in person. Because the call and texts came from different numbers, I was even more confused about tracking this girl down. I was good at a lot of things, but technology wasn't one of them. Normally, Hunter was my go-to person for things like this, but obviously not this time. Stan took the phone and got busy. His brow wrinkled as he worked, tapping and swiping away. It wasn't long before he handed it back to me.

"Man, these kids are smart," he said, shaking his head and taking a sip of his beer. "You're not going to be able to track either number. Well, you can, but it's not going to tell you anything."

"What do you mean?"

"She's calling you from her phone, but doing it through a burner app to make sure her real number stays hidden."

"What's a burner app?"

"Basically, it's a disposable phone number, but on your phone." I raised my eyebrows at him. I still wasn't following. "Let me put it to you this way—it's like having a phone within a phone. You use the app to make the calls or texts, and it gives you an anonymous number. Changes every time you use it if you want. You can also route all your outgoing calls through it, and then there's no way to trace it back to your actual number. There are all kinds of different ones you can use, and that's definitely what she's doing."

"I had no idea you could do all that."

"Yeah, well, those kids sure do. Scary world we live in these days."

I couldn't help but agree. "I don't know what to do now."

He raised his shoulders sheepishly. "Maybe just let it go, unless you hear from her again? I get that you're upset, but you followed the protocol. You did what you could to help." I'd heard those words before—they took me right back to those awful months after my sister passed—and I still wasn't ready to accept them.

"I wish I could, but I can't." I completely understood why you weren't supposed to counsel anyone you knew. Even with only a few details, I was forming a picture of this girl in my mind, starting to feel attached. I was never breaking the rules again. "She's just a kid. I feel too indebted to the parents. What will they think if I don't do everything I can to make sure she's safe? To stop whatever she's planning?"

He nodded his head in understanding. "It's so crazy you ended up with someone from Hunter's school. I mean, I know it's possible, but still. Must feel so weird. Have you talked to him?"

"I asked him if he knew about any videos circulating around his school, and he said no. I was hoping he might've seen it or that someone had sent it to him, but no such luck." I frowned. My brain was racing for solutions. There had to be a way to keep everyone safe.

"Maybe you should ask him again," Stan said, motioning to the bartender for another beer.

I gave him a strange look. "I guess I could. It was early this morning. Maybe he forgot, or he wasn't fully awake yet?"

He snorted and batted his hand at me. "Please," he said, laughing. "What?"

"Do you know how many times you have to ask teenagers about something before they tell you the truth?" He leaned in closer. "You remember when all those cars were getting broken into over on Third Street and vandalized after the football games? All the kids knew it was happening. Every single one of them. But I couldn't get anybody to talk."

"That's different. You're the police. Of course they're scared of you. They don't want to say anything that might get them into trouble. But I'm his mother. We have a good relationship."

Stan shrugged. "My kids are young, so I don't have any personal experience," he said, taking the final sip of his beer, "but I do know one thing about teenagers—they lie."

CHAPTER FIVE

I hurried out of the bar, and didn't even wait until I got to my car to text her:

Hey! Just checking on you to see if you're okay. Been thinking about you all day.

I had no idea if it would go through. I took my time driving home, replaying my conversation with Stan. Even though he'd gone through my phone for me, I was pretty sure he still thought the whole thing was an elaborate prank. But he hadn't been on the phone with her. He'd only seen the texts, and those didn't convey the desperate emotions in her voice. *How did therapists do this every day?* I wondered. I was exhausted from the past twenty-four hours. This was why I only volunteered once a month.

It'd been so hard in the beginning because it brought all my feelings about Holly to the surface, but it had propelled me to face them, exactly like my therapist had predicted. Sometimes it still did; I had just learned how to work through my emotions. But it wasn't only that. Being with others in their pain, especially the kind of pain people were experiencing when they called the center, was tough. I used to get sick every Monday after my weekend shifts. It was like my body's way of shutting down to process things. I'd probably get sick once all this was over.

I pulled into the driveway just as my phone vibrated with a text. I looked down. It was an unknown number. Was it her? Adrenaline tensed my muscles. The exhaustion gone that quickly.

Hi

Are you okay?

She sent a shrugging emoji.

Have you talked to anyone else today? Told them about how you're feeling? It could be too much too soon, but every minute counted when it might be our last conversation.

I don't want to talk to anyone. I don't want to see anyone. I just want everything to be over.

I understood how she felt. I'd gone to grief counseling after my sister died, because no matter what anyone else said, I just didn't get it. My sister was happy. She loved life. She had a family that cared for her and if she'd reached out to any of us, we'd have parted the ocean to save her. My therapist explained that depression was a cunning beast, and it could sneak up on you slowly. It didn't always happen like you might see it portrayed in media: visible despair, days in bed, withdrawing from life. There was a kind of depression that couldn't stop moving or working. That got up every day and wore a big smile so the ones the person loved didn't worry. The depression that needed more and more until it became intolerable, like being force-fed something you could no longer keep down. And in that moment, the person didn't want to die—they just wanted to feel nothing. That stuck with me. It was hard enough getting adults to see a future outside of that moment, and getting a teenager to do that was going to be almost impossible. Teens lived in a world where the future didn't exist.

But I had to try. I wrote back:

I know right now it feels like this experience is going to ruin your life and things will never change; that there's no way out, but I promise you things can change and you won't always feel this way.

You're just saying that bc you're an adult and you have to

No, I'm not. I know what it feels like to be trapped in a really dark place. To feel powerless. I've been there.

I stared at my words after I'd sent them. The truth was I didn't know the right thing to say in this moment. So I gave her the only thing I had—my lived experience. I could feel her staring at the words, too. Wondering what she should say. How she should respond. Finally, her text bubbles, then:

Did something happen to you?

My thumbs hovered on the keyboard. I was about to tell a stranger my darkest secret. What was I doing? I shoved the fears down. If I was going to ask her to be brave, then I had to be brave, too.

Can you call me?

A call from another unknown number flashed across my screen immediately.

CHLOE: [awkward and hesitant] Hey . . .

FELICIA: Hi, uh, thanks for calling. It's a lot to write out in a text and it's good to hear your voice.

CHLOE: You sound different.

FELICIA: What do you mean?

CHLOE: You sounded different on the phone last night.

FELICIA: I did?

CHLOE: Mm-hmmm . . .

FELICIA: Maybe it's because I was using a headset and I'm on a computer when I'm at the center.

CHLOE: Right. Is that the something bad that happened to you—someone committed suicide? Is that why you work there?

FELICIA: Well—my sister died by suicide, so that's why I started working there. You're right about that. But that's not what I'm talking about. That's not why I can relate to what you're going through.

CHLOE: It's not? What happened to you?

FELICIA: [deep breath] I was assaulted by a boyfriend seventeen years ago, and he almost killed me. It's not exactly the same situation as you. I get that. Nobody recorded the incident and sent it around to other people. I don't understand that part, and I know it must add a whole other level of pain to the experience . . . but I do know what it's like to have your innocence completely stripped away from you in an instant. To have something so traumatic happen to you that nothing feels real afterward. I know what it's like to spend all your time wishing for a life you know you'll never get back. To feel alone and want to die from the shame and embarrassment. But nothing was worse than not feeling safe, and—

CHLOE: YES! I never stop being scared. I can't eat. I can't sleep. I can't do anything. When I try to sleep, I just have these awful nightmares. I see stuff—what they did to me, them laughing—whenever I close my eyes. It's like they're watching me. Still. And I'm just terrified. I'm so tired of being scared. I—I don't want to feel like this anymore.

FELICIA: I understand. I really do. And I promise it goes away eventually. It does. You learn how to feel safe again. It just takes awhile. And the key thing is, you've got to have people around you that can love you and support you through it.

CHLOE: So you told people what happened to you?

FELICIA: I did.

CHLOE: I'm such an idiot. I should've listened to my mom. I wasn't supposed to go to that stupid party and I did anyway. That's what I get.

FELICIA: Oh, honey. Whatever happened wasn't your fault.

CHLOE: Yes, it was. I wasn't supposed to be there, and if I'd just done what my parents told me to do, then none of this would be happening. It's all my fault!

FELICIA: I want you to know that I'm a parent, too, and I'd want my child to tell me if something awful happened to them so that I could help them. Even if they'd done something they weren't supposed to do. Seriously. I'd just want to be there for them no matter what. I'm sure your parents feel the same way.

CHLOE: You don't know my parents.

FELICIA: You're right, I don't. But it might help just to get it out.

[Long pause]

CHLOE: Well, maybe I could tell you . . . Do you want to know what happened?

FELICIA: Only if you want to tell me.

CHLOE: Promise you won't tell anyone?

FELICIA: Your secret is safe with me.

CHLOE: Okay . . . [deep exhale] . . . There's this guy I have a huge crush on, but he's a senior, and I'm a freshman, so my parents would never let me hang out with him. They'd totally freak if they knew we were even talking.

He's one of those guys that got held back for sports, so he's about to turn nineteen, you know? My best friend's talking to one of his friends, too. Anyway, there was this huge party after the Worthington football game, and we were, like, two of the only freshman girls invited. Everyone else was basically juniors and seniors. [another pause] I told my parents I was sleeping over at her house, and she told her parents she was sleeping over at mine, so we could go to the party. I never should've gone . . .

FELICIA: Whose party? The boy you had a crush on?

CHLOE: No, it wasn't at his house. It was at this kid Jett's. He has all the parties after the football games. Everybody goes. [sniffles] Anyway, everything was fine in the beginning, you know? It was just like a regular party. People were having fun. But then my friend got superdrunk, like, sloppy, you know what I mean? So, I pretty much just had to take care of her. And before you get all judgy—I didn't drink anything.

FELICIA: I would never judge you. I'm just here to listen, and help.

CHLOE: Well, just so you know, I never drink alcohol—it's gross, and it makes me feel disgusting. I drank Sprite the entire night. Anyway, one minute we were in the living room dancing and acting like idiots. I remember that clearly. And then the next thing I remember is . . . what I remember is . . . being on my stomach on a bed. Someone was, you know . . . behind me, they were . . . they were . . . [sobbing]

FELICIA: It's okay, honey. It's okay. You don't have to say it.

CHLOE: I wish I was as drunk as my friend. She doesn't remember any of it. Not a single thing. They drugged her, too, but she was already blacked out by the time we got upstairs, so the whole night is gone. She doesn't have any pieces. The only reason she knows it happened is because I told her. [pauses] Well, and the stupid video. She's seen that, too. She was in the room with me, but she's not on the video. For some reason, they decided to just film me. Guess I was special. [snort]

FELICIA: Do you know how many people there were? In the room?

CHLOE: Four? Maybe five? Might've been more. . . . I was terrified when I came to, and started trying to fight them off me. I kept kicking. Biting. Scratching. All that. But it was like my legs and my arms didn't work right. Everything was floppy and uncoordinated. I guess it was because of the drugs they gave me or whatever. But I tried to fight them off me. Then I was stumbling around the room naked. I remember screaming for my clothes, bumping into things. I was so confused and disoriented. I thought—I thought my friend was dead. She wasn't moving, just lying there face down on the bed with her arm flopped to the side. At first, I thought the guy behind her was trying to help her, and it took me a second to figure out what was really happening. What he was doing to her. I tried to get him off her, but he just threw me down, and I cracked my head on the floor. It was so hard to work my body. They all just stood around, laughing. That's what they filmed. Someone filmed me freaking out . . . [starts crying softly]

FELICIA: Oh my god. I'm so sorry you were hurt like that. [long pause] Was this the guy you had a crush on? The one that pushed you?

CHLOE: [still crying] No, it wasn't him. He left the party early because he was going on a college visit in the morning; he needed to get up at six or something crazy like that. But still, I'm sure he saw the video, and he's never going to want anything to do with me now. Nobody is. So, that's why I have to make them pay. [pause] You know what I was thinking today? I'm not sure I want to shoot them. If I shoot them, then they're just dead in a second. That's too easy. I want them to suffer. Really suffer.

FELICIA: [sudden change in her tone of voice, wavering] That's understandable . . .

CHLOE: What's wrong? You sound funny. Are you going to tell someone? You promised you wouldn't tell anyone!

FELICIA: No, no, it's not that. I'm sorry. I told you—I'm not going to tell anyone what we've talked about, okay?

CHLOE: Promise?

FELICIA: Yes. If—if I sound a little distracted, it's just because my boss keeps blowing up my phone.

CHLOE: Oh. Do you have to go?

FELICIA: I hate to do this to you, sweetie, I really do, but I think I have to take his call. He says it's an emergency. I feel awful cutting this short. Are you going to be okay? Can we talk later?

CHLOE: I'm not sure if I'll be able to talk later.

FELICIA: Okay, well, if you can't talk later, promise me that you'll call or text me tomorrow? We can figure this out together. I promised to keep your secret, so you've got to give me your word that we'll talk again soon.

CHLOE: Okay . . . I promise.

FELICIA: All right. Just remember that I care about you. And we'll talk soon. I have to go now.

I hated lying to her, but I didn't know what else to do. I had to get off the line. My hands shook. I dropped the phone on my lap and rubbed my face. My brain scrambled to make sense of things. It had been so difficult to feign ignorance for the second half of the call. Ever since she confessed to being at Jett's party.

I knew Jett Frasier. He was on the cross-country team. And Hunter had been at the same party.

CHAPTER SIX

I sat frozen in the car and staring at my phone. I was still in the driveway since I'd hung up with the girl ten minutes ago, but I couldn't bring myself to go in the house. Not yet.

If what she said was true—that she and her friend were the only two freshmen there—then all I had to do was go inside and ask Hunter about it. On the one hand, I was grateful to have a way forward. If I knew who she was, I could easily find her parents by using the Buckley family directory and tell them what was happening. As relieved as that made me, I was equally troubled that Hunter was there. Could he or one of his friends be involved in any way?

Except I'd asked him about the video, and he said he hadn't seen anything. Could he have been there and not been involved? Those parties were pretty big. Was it possible he had no idea it happened? Actually had not seen the video? I wanted that to be the case, but it seemed highly unlikely. My thoughts spun. I was so torn.

But that wasn't even the thing that bothered me the most.

I couldn't get past her mention of the college visit her crush was supposed to go on—a detail I also knew something about. This was the trip planned for all the junior and senior athletes to check out Stout's athletic department. Hunter was supposed to go on the same visit. It was the reason he'd planned to stay overnight at his best friend Shai's house after the party. But that's not what happened: he called me in the middle of the night and asked me to come pick him up. He'd gotten into my car reeking of alcohol with an angry red scar on his cheek. The same night she got assaulted.

Hunter couldn't really have had anything to do with that girl's assault, could he? It had to be a coincidence. It had to be. That's what I kept telling myself as I finally forced myself to get out of the car and go into the house.

"I'm in the kitchen, Mom," Hunter yelled when he heard me come in.

My stomach rolled.

The sound of his familiar voice, calling out so sweetly like he'd done hundreds of times, sent a chill through my body. A sense of impending doom filled the air. I took tentative steps through the living room and into the kitchen. I wanted to know the truth as much as I wanted to stay in denial. Whatever happened next, I knew I could never go back.

Hunter's back was to me at the stove. He turned around and flashed me a quick smile. "I was starving, so I started dinner. It's just pasta, but don't worry, I've got broccoli on, too," he said, pointing to the steamer on the counter.

"Thanks," I said. My voice didn't sound like me, but he acted like he didn't notice and turned around to finish cooking. I stared at his back as he stirred the noodles in the pot. It felt like just yesterday he was a little kid, sitting in a high chair—and now, here he was, taking care of himself, almost an adult.

The scene from the night of the party played out again while I watched him cook.

I'd fallen asleep in front of the TV when his text woke me up at almost two a.m. My brain immediately flipped through awful scenarios—car accidents, hospitals, sudden sickness—and I sat straight up in bed, immediately texting him back. I breathed a sigh of relief when he said he was okay and just wanted me to come pick him up. He couldn't fall asleep at Shai's house and wanted to spend the night in his own bed.

I was already up and moving through the house before I'd finished reading his text, slipping on my shoes and searching for my car keys. I was surprised when he wrote that he was actually not at Shai's but at the water tower. They'd gone to a party after the football game, and Shai's parents were supposed to pick them up afterward. What was he doing out by the water tower? It wasn't anywhere near Shai's house. The old Clark County water tower still stood outside the elementary school on Seventh Street, right next to the cornfields. It'd been there since I was a kid, a historic landmark. Kids climbed up it all the time—it was incredibly dangerous, but it was a rite of passage in his childhood same as it had been in mine.

I was in the car and headed to him in less than a minute. I didn't like the idea of him at the water tower all by himself in the middle of the night. It didn't matter that he was over six feet tall and seventeen—he was still my baby.

I didn't see him when I first pulled up, but it wasn't long before he appeared out of the shadows and slid into the passenger seat. I immediately smelled alcohol on him.

"You stink," I said. It wasn't just the alcohol . . . he reeked of sweat, like he did when I picked him up after cross-country practice.

He grunted without looking up from his phone. His hair was greasy and hanging in his eyes. Then I saw the huge scratch on his neck. Right on his jawline.

"Jesus, what happened to your neck?" I asked, reaching over to brush his hair off his face so I could see it better. But he smacked my hand away.

"Nothing. Don't touch it. Leave me alone." He glared at me. Was that a mark on his cheek, too?

"Hunter, what's going on? What happened tonight?" He'd never been in any sort of trouble before. He wasn't that kind of kid. But none of this felt right.

"Nothing, Mom. Everything's fine. I went for a walk and ended up here. That's all." He hunched over in the passenger seat, typing fast on his phone. "I told you, I just changed my mind about sleeping over. I want to sleep in my own bed."

"Everything's obviously not fine. You call me in the middle of the night to pick you up at the water tower, and you get in my car smelling like alcohol, looking all ragged with a big scratch on your neck? Come on, Hunter. I'm not stupid." The car was starting to warm up, but my words still came out in white puffs.

I wasn't a blind-eye, bury-your-head-in-the-sand kind of parent. I was a tell-me-like-it-is type so we can figure out the problem together, and losing my sister had made me even more hypervigilant. Kids got into all kinds of trouble growing up, especially the older they got. My goal as a parent was to be his first call if he needed help or if he was in trouble. I'd gotten something right, because I was here, but I wanted to know what was going on. Clearly, this was more than feeling like sleeping in his own bed.

"I already told you—nothing. I just wanna go home. Can you leave me alone?"

"No, Hunter. I can't. Obviously, something happened tonight." I reached for his phone like I was going to take it away, since it was the only leverage I had left with him. He pulled it protectively against his chest, understanding the implied threat.

"Fine," he huffed, finally looking up. "Me and Shai got into a fight. Happy now?" He scowled at me. There was no mistaking the angry red mark on his cheek.

"Like, an actual physical fight?" They'd never been in a fight, and they'd been best friends since Shai moved to town in second grade. He was taller than Hunter and weighed twenty pounds more, but my nickname for him was Gentle Giant. He was so mellow and never got riled. He was the calm to Hunter's storm.

"Yes, Mom," he said with the classic teenage sigh like I might be the most annoying person in the world with all my questions, but I didn't care. I wasn't letting something like this go.

"What did you get in a fight about?" Hunter had never been in a physical altercation with anyone. He had a temper, but he wasn't a fighter. Something must've set him off. I waited a few more beats, but he ignored me. "What was the fight about?" I repeated myself.

"Nothing, okay? Just stupid shit. Don't worry about it. I just wanna go home, and go to bed." He pulled his AirPods out of his pocket and popped them in his ears. His face closed; completely impassive.

I dropped it then. Not because I didn't want to know more, but because I knew pushing him would've gotten us nowhere. It was late, and we were both tired. Talking to him when he was in that kind of a foul mood was pointless.

I brought it up one more time at breakfast the next morning. I gave him an earful about making responsible choices when he was drinking, like I'd been doing ever since he started this past summer. He was seventeen, and I wasn't naïve enough to think he wasn't going to experiment with alcohol. I secretly hoped he chose alcohol over all the other terrifying substances kids could get their hands on these days. We reviewed the rules—never drinking when he had to drive, the importance of pacing yourself and stopping before you're too drunk, calling me if he got in trouble—and then I asked him about the fight again. He didn't want to talk about it in the morning any more than he'd wanted to talk the night before, but I didn't let him wriggle his way out of it that time.

"Is that why you and Shai fought? Were you drunk?" I asked, refusing to let it go.

"It was just a dumb fight over a girl, Mom, okay? Just let it be. We're fine. You're making it into a way bigger deal than it needs to be."

I wanted to ask which girl, but talking about girls was sure to shut him down completely. We could talk about almost anything, but for some reason, he didn't like telling me about any of his girlfriends or the things that happened with them. Elaine, my friend from the call center, assured me her boys were the same way when they were his age, and they shared all that stuff with her husband instead. I hoped Hunter was talking to one of his coaches or his friends' dads about it. Being left out of that part of his life still hurt, though. He didn't even tell me when he got his first girlfriend. I found out on Instagram, when she posted a picture of the two of them together and I saw him tagged.

"I just can't believe you and Shai actually fought. Did he hit you?" The mark on his cheek had grown into a bruise in the morning, and the scratch on his neck was still red and inflamed.

"It wasn't like we boxed each other. He just kinda smacked me." He scarfed down his bowl of cereal like he hadn't eaten in days, then poured himself a second. The boy could eat.

"And did you hit him back?" Hunter had only hit someone once, and it was in kindergarten. Since childhood, he'd never done anything violent or showed the slightest sign of aggression,

I was sure of it. I'd been watching for signs since he was born. And I breathed a sigh of relief as each year passed and they weren't there. I refused to believe this was the first sign after all that time. There had to be another explanation.

"No, I didn't hit him," he said, like it was a stupid question.

We left it alone after that, and I'd barely thought about it since. Hunter and Shai carried on like nothing had happened, so I figured whatever it was, they'd worked it out by themselves.

But all of this came flooding back now, as I watched Hunter prepare our dinner. I shoved my feelings down and eased my way into the conversation.

"Hey, Hunter, do you know if Jett's dad was there at the last party he had?" I asked.

"Jett's party?" he asked without turning around. "He hasn't had one since the Worthington game."

"I know," I said. "That's the one I'm asking about."

He shrugged, turning around and bringing a plate of bread over to the table. "I don't know. That was, like, weeks ago. And his dad just hides in his office, anyway."

That's why I always warned Hunter about making good choices, especially while he was at Jett's. It was the boys' favorite hangout spot because his house was the biggest and the least supervised. His dad was a single parent like me, but that's where our similarities stopped. He was an e-trader who practically worked around the clock. He spent most of his time tucked away upstairs in his office, oblivious to anything happening in the rest of the house.

I grabbed a piece of bread even though the thought of food made me nauseous. I tried to act nonchalant. "Wasn't that the night I picked you up from the water tower? When you were supposed to spend the night at Shai's?"

He froze, just for a second, but long enough for me to notice. Then he quickly shrugged again, dismissing it. "Maybe. I mean, it could've been. I told you, I don't remember."

He hurried over to the sink. He drained the pasta like I'd taught him all those years ago. My being a single mom meant he knew how to do all kinds of things around the house—cooking, cleaning, laundry. It'd started when he was young—not out of any old-school you'll-carry-your-weight-around-the-house attitude, but out of pure necessity. By now, he was more comfortable in our kitchen than I was, and he was on his way to becoming a better cook, too.

Was it a coincidence that he and Shai got into a fight the same night the girl was assaulted? I desperately wanted it to be, but what were the chances? There were too many coincidences stacked upon each other.

"But wasn't that party the same night you got in the fight with Shai?" I asked as he sprinkled Parmesan on the noodles.

"I don't know. I haven't even thought about the fight with Shai since it happened. It was so stupid." He carried the dishes to the table and set a plate in front of me. "What do you want to drink?"

He dismissed it that quickly, but something wasn't right. I felt it, the way it curled my guts, and a mother's instinct is never wrong.

CHAPTER SEVEN

I lay in bed, staring at the ceiling, unable to sleep. It'd been that way for the last three hours. If I didn't fall asleep soon, I knew I'd have to give up on the idea of sleep altogether and just get up to start my day.

Even though Hunter acted like he didn't remember the night of the party or anything that happened, I couldn't shake the feeling he wasn't telling me the truth. It had awakened my deepest fears. The ones I usually kept at bay, but that pushed their way to the surface late at night, or when I was overtired. Tonight both were true, and my fears had left me in a cold sweat, tossing and turning.

Lots of women called themselves single parents after they got divorced, but I was the real deal. I'd never been married, and Hunter didn't have any kind of relationship with his dad. He'd never even met him. He barely knew who he was.

And all of that was intentional.

Because Hunter's dad was a scary, violent man. One I'd put in prison for life with no chance of parole, which was the only reason I didn't live in fear every single day. He was the one who attacked me, left me bleeding at the bottom of a staircase. The one I had called my boyfriend when I was on the phone with the girl—but really, he was a cautionary tale against one-night stands.

The day my world changed forever started like any other day. I was fresh out of law school and had just started working as a clerk down at city hall. After work, a colleague and I went out for drinks at our favorite bar. That's where I met James. He sauntered up to our table in his low-slung jeans and his tight T-shirt, clearly selected to show off all his muscles.

"Can I buy you a drink?" he asked boldly. Long dark lashes housed his dreamy eyes, and he had a crooked, irresistible grin.

There was an instant spark, which was all I cared about then. I was completely focused on my career and wasn't interested in anything more than a little fun, and James and I had plenty of it that night. Drinking. Flirting. Laughing. He was only in town for the night on business, so he was perfect for a no-strings-attached situation. We hung out at the bar until it closed and stumbled down the street to his hotel afterward. I told him goodbye in the morning, and didn't think I'd ever see him again.

But then I missed my period at the end of the month. I was working superlong days, barely sleeping, and surviving on coffee and protein bars, so it never occurred to me that the disruption in my cycle was anything but stress-related. Besides, I was diligent about birth control. But then I missed my next period, too, and I started having episodes of being so tired I could barely keep my eyes open. I'd be in court and suddenly feel like I got injected with tranquilizers. It took all my willpower to stay awake. I went to see my doctor because I was scared something was seriously wrong with me.

She wore a tiny smile on her face when she came back into the room with my blood test results. "Well, you're not dying, so that's good. But you are pregnant." She shrugged noncommittally, unsure how I'd feel about the news and giving me space to process.

I was shocked. I shook my head at her. "That's impossible. I'm on birth control, and the last time I had sex, I used a condom, too."

I made her run the pregnancy test again, convinced there'd been a mistake, but the next one came back just as positive. So did the three at-home pregnancy tests I took that night. I was stunned. I'd always wanted to be a mother—it was one of the top three goals on my list of ambitions. But I wanted to do lots of other things before getting to it. I had a well-drawn-out plan for my life, and so far, I'd been following it to a T. An unplanned pregnancy from a one-night stand did not fit with that timeline.

I spent the next few days walking around in shock, but it wasn't long before the shock grew into excitement. I still didn't feel like it was the perfect time to have a baby, but the universe clearly had other plans. Pregnant, after using the pill *and* a condom? It felt a bit too miraculous. Divinely inspired. After that, my anticipation and excitement grew every day along with the baby.

I toyed with not telling James. After all, he was basically a stranger to me, and I was ready to take this on alone. I hadn't seen him since the night we hooked up and we'd only exchanged a couple funny texts since then. But I figured it was the right thing to do. I didn't expect him to be a part of the kid's life, and I wasn't sure if I even wanted him to be, but giving him a choice was the responsible adult thing to do, so I did it. I made it clear from the moment I told him that he was under no obligation to help me care for the baby. His response was shocking.

"Are you kidding?" He was back in town for work again, and we were at a restaurant called Mahogany's. He jumped up from our table and raced around to grab me. He swooped me up and twirled me around. We spun until we were dizzy and he plopped me back down with a huge grin on his face. "I'm so excited, I don't know what to do with myself. This is the best news!"

And he wasn't kidding. He was over the moon about becoming a dad, and about being with me. He kept saying it was destiny because of the circumstances, and it was hard not to be moved by his enthusiasm. He made it clear he was serious about me and immediately started showering me with love and attention. Nobody had ever been that into me before, and it was incredibly mesmerizing and intoxicating. He called and checked up on me constantly, sending me flowers and meals. Cute notes at work. I'd never been a romantic—still wasn't—but he swept me off my feet. Charmed the pants off me. Love-bombed me, even though I'd never heard the term at the time.

But then everything changed when he moved to Wisconsin.

He turned possessive the moment he stepped foot in Eagle Rock. He wanted to move in together right away, but to me it felt way too fast, even though we were having a baby together. We'd never even been on an official first date, besides the night we went out to dinner and I told him about the pregnancy. He wanted to know where I was going, what I was doing, and who I was with every moment of the day. He was jealous of any attention people gave me, and was convinced everyone I met wanted to sleep with me. He didn't even like me talking to my parents or my sister. It was one red flag after another, and I pulled back immediately. That's when things got scary.

I tried ending the relationship over the phone as delicately as possible, stressing that we'd moved too fast with things. "You're more than welcome to be in the baby's life if you still want to be and we can talk about what that might look like, but I'm not interested in a romantic relationship." I knew exactly what I wanted to say and stuck to the script. I tried to keep my tone upbeat and light, as if we were any other couple that just hadn't worked out.

"Oh, so you just used me to get pregnant, then? Is that it? You needed some kind of sperm donor? All you bitches are the same." He said it like he was disgusted with me. His words were short and clipped. "I gave up my entire life for you, you know that? All the sacrifices I've made to be with you and this baby? Moving here. Taking care of you. Trying to give you everything so we can be a family. How dare you?" I couldn't see him, but I could feel his rage through the phone, and I didn't like it. "You're not getting away with this. All you conniving bitches think you can just play us. That's not going to happen. Not this time."

None of what he was saying was based in reality, and I was terrified. He spoke like we'd been together for years rather than seven weeks, and his sweeping statements about women were shocking. But it was his anger that scared me the most.

That's when I did a thorough background search on James.

Turned out, he'd always lived in Wisconsin, only a few hours away from Eagle Rock. His story about being a financial broker in New Jersey was a complete lie, much like everything else he'd told me that night at the bar. He had a criminal record spanning the last ten years: domestic violence and assault, drunk driving, aggravated assault, aggravated robbery. And those were just his felonies. He had misdemeanors spanning all the way back to his adolescence. He'd been in jail multiple times and served three years in prison. I was horrified, and the shame of being an intelligent and successful woman that had fallen for someone so awful was one of the hardest parts.

I went no-contact immediately after that phone call, but that didn't stop him. I'd never forget the fury burning in his eyes when he showed up at my apartment unannounced and uninvited, and told me I couldn't escape him. Or the way he had looked when he grabbed me by my hair and shoved me down four flights of stairs after I refused to talk to him or let him inside my place. I'd never been hit in my life, and even knowing what I knew about him, the punch to my face was a total shock. If it hadn't been for my friend

June worrying because I didn't text her when I got inside, I probably would've died at the bottom of those stairs that night. I'm sure that's what he intended.

Police officers camped outside my hospital room as the doctors and nurses tended to my injuries and did everything they could to save the baby. The trauma had sent him into distress. They found James at the bar where we'd met, drinking and carrying on as if he hadn't just tried to kill me. I never went back to my apartment. I stayed with my parents until he was officially incarcerated. I was his third strike, and in the state of Wisconsin, that meant life without parole. I read my victim statement at his sentencing hearing, and I never saw or heard from him again.

But that didn't mean I didn't think about him. A violent monster was Hunter's biological father, and no matter how hard I tried to forget that, it was always there, lurking under the surface. I never told Hunter the truth about his dad. It was the only secret I kept from him, but I didn't want him to know where he came from. Instead, I told him his dad died before he was born. Maybe that made me a terrible mother, but I didn't think so. Not when I was doing it to protect him.

When he got old enough to start asking questions, I came up with a plan. My friend Nick had gone into the military and died in Iraq. It happened when Hunter was a baby, so I told him Nick was his dad. My family and friends supported the idea. It was easier that way, and it assured that if there ever came a day when Hunter decided to check up on my story about his dad, there would be a man there when he looked. I even had a couple pictures of Nick and me together. I'd never felt guilty about it. Still didn't. Hunter's life was better thinking he came from two people that loved him.

I watched him like a hawk when he was younger, especially at the playground with other kids, analyzing his every move for the slightest sign that he'd inherited his father's violent tendencies. What would he do when he was provoked? Did he lash out? Did he like hurting other kids? I thought of his predisposition to violence like any other developmental disorder—early intervention was key. If there was anything there, I was going to spot it and treat it right away.

But that's the thing: there was never anything there. He had always been the sweetest kid. I waited for him to shove kids down the slide or hit them with sticks when he was mad, but he was the one who helped his friends up after they fell down, the one running to defend his friends against bullying. Over the years, I'd slowly relaxed and quit holding my breath and waiting to see if he was okay. I stopped analyzing everything he did. And there'd never been a single alarming sign.

Until now.

What really happened that night at the party?

After I picked Hunter up from the water tower, I never thought to check on his story. I trusted him. I always had. He'd never given me a reason not to. As he moved from middle school into high school, we had all kinds of conversations about the importance of me being able to trust him. And that in order for me to trust him, he needed to tell me the truth about things, even stuff that might get him in trouble. He'd never been in any serious trouble, though. Not at home or school. The worst thing he'd done was skip school to go to Noah's Ark, the water park not far from where we live. He went with an entire crew of kids, which pretty much ensured they'd get caught—a reckless move, but hardly concerning. Beyond that? Eye rolls and a bratty attitude when I asked him to get off his phone or was nagging him about college applications were as far as his acting out went. He was a good kid. I knew he was.

I never checked with Shai's mom, Ruby, about what happened either, and maybe I should have. I wasn't close with her—I'd pulled way back on conversations with Hunter's friends' parents over the years, especially in the last few as he started developing his independence. He didn't need or want me micromanaging his life, and as hard as it was for me to let go, he was right. He had to learn how to do things on his own and navigate situations without me acting as a buffer.

But the two of them getting into a fight was a big deal, and it *was* strange Ruby hadn't said anything to me about it. I'd just run into her at the grocery store last week. Wouldn't she have at least mentioned it? Like, "Hey, how crazy is it that the boys got into a fight?" or something like that?

Except I hadn't said anything about it either. And not on purpose. It'd just never crossed my mind when I saw her. Maybe it was the same for her.

It was also possible she just didn't know about it, and I didn't want to overstep. But then what did she think when Hunter wasn't there in the morning when they were supposed to leave for the college visit? I decided I was calling her as soon as it was a decent hour. I rolled out of bed and sat up, anxiously rubbing my face. There was no chance I was sleeping tonight. I was shocked when my phone buzzed with a text. Was it her? I hated not being able to save her contact information.

I can't sleep

What a coincidence, I wrote back, I can't either

Omg you're up. I never thought you'd be up!!! Can I call you?

Of course. You can always call me. That's why I gave you my number.

I headed downstairs to make coffee as I answered her call.

FELICIA: Hey, hon, I'm sorry you can't sleep.

CHLOE: I never sleep anymore.

FELICIA: You will again someday, I promise. It just doesn't feel like it right now.

CHLOE: How do you know all this stuff?

FELICIA: I told you, I've been through it. All of it. Not just the incident, but everything that happens afterward. The stuff people don't talk about. You know, I slept in my closet for two months after my attack. With a bat in one hand and pepper spray in the other.

CHLOE: *Really?* [deep sigh] I kinda like knowing there's someone else that's been through it.

FELICIA: There's lots of us. You'd be surprised. I know you feel all alone and that there's nobody else in the world right now that gets it, but other people *have* been through what you've been through. Maybe not exactly the same, but there are so many sexual assault survivors. If we looked, we could probably find a support group for you somewhere. I bet they have one just for teenagers.

CHLOE: I keep trying to talk to my friend about what happened, the one who was there, but she doesn't want to talk about it. She wants to pretend like it never happened. Which I get. Totally easy for her, right? She remembers nothing and she wasn't in the video, so her life isn't ruined. You know what's wild? She acts like *I* made it all up. Looks at me like I'm crazy.

FELICIA: I'm sorry she's treating you that way. Her response doesn't have anything to do with you, though, you know that, right? She's trying to keep herself safe. That kind of thinking protects her from having to admit the same thing happened to her.

CHLOE: I hate it. It's like she doesn't even want to talk to me. Not just about what happened. She's practically ignoring me right now. Like, normally I'd be calling her, but instead I'm calling some old lady I don't even know. I– Oh my god, I'm sorry, I didn't mean to– I was just . . .

FELICIA: [laughing] It's okay, I get it. Trust me, I understand we're in kind of a strange situation here, and I'm just glad you have someone to talk to, even if it is just some old lady.

[Small laugh from Chloe. Long pause]

FELICIA: Does anything help get you to sleep?

CHLOE: Thinking about what I'm going to do to them. Sometimes that's the only thing that helps. But I just get really scared. [pauses] Did that ever happen to you? Like, you feel like it's happening to you again, right in the moment?

FELICIA: Sometimes. There's a word for that, you know? It's called PTSD. Lots of people have it after they experience a traumatic event. I did. For a long time. Like I said, sometimes I still do, but it gets better over time. I know I keep saying that, but it's only because I know it's true, and if you can just hold on long enough to get there, it'll happen for you, too. It won't always hurt this bad.

CHLOE: Sometimes it gets so bad I don't think I'm going to be able to stand it. That's when I close my eyes supertight and I just picture myself shooting them in their faces over and over again. It's this violent scene I let play out but it calms me down.

FELICIA: [swallows hard] I understand.

[soft sniffles]

CHLOE: I don't know how I'm going to make it through tonight.

FELICIA: Do you like baths?

CHLOE: Um, yeah, sometimes.

FELICIA: What if you just got in the bath?

CHLOE: I guess I could . . .

FELICIA: Why don't you try that? Just soak. Let the water hold you for a minute.

[pause]

CHLOE: Okay . . . I'm gonna go.

FELICIA: Text me in a few hours and let me know how you're feeling, okay?

But there was nobody on the other end. She was already gone. Had she gotten into the bathtub, or gone for the gun?

A pit opened in my stomach.

A bath wasn't going to help her with anything. Not really, but I was running out of things to say. I wanted to tell her how many nights I spent plotting James's death while he was in prison. Imagining what I would do—how badly I'd torture him—if they found him not guilty, or if his lawyer could somehow get him out of there. The only reason I was able to live freely now was that my attacker couldn't hurt me any longer. If he hadn't landed in prison without parole? I might've taken matters into my own hands.

But I didn't tell her that. I couldn't. No matter how much I wanted to bury it, to return to the life we'd lived just twenty-four hours before, I couldn't deny that we might be talking about my son.

CHAPTER EIGHT

I waited until five minutes after eight, and then I called Shai's mom. "Hey, Ruby," I said when she picked up. I'd texted her earlier to see if she could talk.

"Hi, Felicia, is something wrong? Your text kinda freaked me out."

I laughed nervously. I didn't want to be doing this. It was silly. It didn't seem nearly as serious in the light of day. Lots of drama happened at teenage parties, right? Just because Shai and Hunter got into a fight on the same night as the girl's attack didn't mean those two things were connected. That's what I'd kept telling myself. "Actually, I've been meaning to call you for a couple weeks. You've been on my to-do list! But I've had a huge trial, so I've been working eighteen-hour days."

"Oh gosh, I don't know how you do it," she said. "What's up?"

"Do you remember the night of the Worthington football game?"

"The Worthington football game?" She considers it. "You mean, did I go?"

"No, just, do you remember that night? The boys went to a party after the football game, and planned to stay the night over at your house? They had the trip to Stout in the morning." I tried to prompt her memory, hoping she could provide me with some clues to put my mind to rest. I had to find some peace. Some kind of resolution. I couldn't keep living like this.

"The one where they all wore their pajamas?"

"No, I think that was the following week."

She laughed. "Jeez. These kids have quite the social life, huh?"

"They're definitely living their best lives, that's for sure." I laughed in return. "The reason I was asking about it is because Hunter was supposed to stay over with you, and I guess him and Shai got into some kind of a fight that night. I ended up coming to pick him up at, like, two in the morning. He looked pretty rough, and he said he wanted to come home because they'd gotten into a fight."

"They're fighting?" she asked in disbelief. "Hunter just stayed here last weekend."

I laughed again. "I know. I guess it's a guy thing, right? Like they can just fight it out and go back to being friends the next day? Apparently, they're not like women, who have to ignore each other for days and turn everyone else against whoever they're mad at, too." I was trying to lighten the mood.

"I had no idea they were fighting," she said.

"I mean, they're not. At least I don't think so. They seem totally fine now," I assured her.

"So they worked it out?"

"Yes."

"I'm sorry, what's the problem then? I'm not sure I'm following you."

I took a deep breath. "I was just wondering if you remembered anything about the fight, or what they fought about. Like I said, I'd wanted to ask you about it before, but I've been so busy I haven't had the opportunity until now."

"When you say 'fight,' do you mean an actual physical fight?"

"Yes, Hunter said he hit him."

"Shai hit Hunter?" she asked incredulously.

"According to Hunter. That's really why I was calling. And don't feel bad, he's totally fine—I was just trying to figure out what happened for the two of them to get into it like that. They've never fought like that before, so I figured it had to be something major. I'm just over here being a private investigator, you know?"

"Hmm . . . that is strange, but if it was the weekend before the pajama party, then I don't think Hunter even came home with Shai. I was out of town on a business trip, and Corbin was the one on kid duty. He would've picked them up, but I'm pretty sure Hunter wasn't with him. Let me text him quick and see . . ."

I waited while she tapped out a text to her husband. My stomach was in knots. I was so torn. I wanted to know, but at the same time I didn't.

"How's the trial going, by the way?" she asked while we waited.

"Oh, you know, the usual hateful drama between divorced couples."

"I don't know how you do it," she said. "That's all I could think about when I was going through mine, all the lawyers that had to live in that world every day. It— Oh!" she exclaimed, interrupting herself. "He texted back. Let me see what he said . . . that's what I thought. He said he picked Shai up from the party, but Hunter wasn't with him. He actually picked him up early because Shai was starting to get one of his migraines. I guess he threw up in the car on the way home. Obviously, a memorable night for Corbin."

My heart sank. "He didn't say anything about Hunter? I mean, Corbin didn't mention if Shai said anything about Hunter that night?"

"Hold on, I'll ask him quick." A few beats passed. "No, sorry, he says he doesn't remember Shai saying anything about Hunter.

Maybe it was some other weekend?" she asked, sensing there was something wrong.

"I don't think so."

"Hmm . . ." she said and it wasn't long before the silence grew awkward. "Wish I could be more helpful."

I quickly responded, projecting all kinds of happiness into my voice like this was perfectly okay, and there was nothing to be concerned about. "No worries. I appreciate you letting me pick your brain about it."

"I'm sure there's a totally reasonable explanation," she said, with way more confidence than I felt.

"Absolutely." I faked optimism. "Maybe things just got out of hand at the party, and he didn't want to tell me about it."

"Exactly. The secret life of teenagers. Blaming it on your best friend. Not a bad choice." Her voice was light, but she was probably going to tell Shai I called and ask him about it. Hunter would be pissed, totally betrayed I'd called someone behind his back. I couldn't believe we were here, but we were.

"Anyway, thanks for all your help."

"No problem, I hope you figure it out."

I sat on the chair staring at the phone after I hung up, but not for long. If Hunter hadn't been with Shai, then where was he? What was he doing at the water tower? When did he leave Jett's house?

No matter which way I looked at it, my son was lying to me.

Something happened at that party.

Could Shai have been one of the boys in the video? Maybe Hunter was bruised up because he helped *end* the attack? He'd done that in kindergarten once, slid underneath a bathroom stall and pushed a kid who was bullying his friend. Maybe he'd saved the girl, and wouldn't tell me because he didn't want to get his other friends in trouble? There were lots of ways he could've been involved. Maybe he was one of the good guys.

I didn't know how that girl's story ended. We'd never reached the part where she got away. What if there'd been a fight then? I just needed more information. I pulled up the last number the mystery girl had texted me from and tapped out a text to her. I didn't know if she'd even get it, since I didn't know how the burner app worked, but it was worth a try.

Hey! Just checking on you to see how you are. Can we talk?

CHAPTER NINE

I'd been obsessively checking my phone since I texted her. Still nothing. But who knows if she even got it. I was grateful for the distraction of work, but by the time I was headed home for the day, all my obsessive worrying was back in full force. What if I never heard from her again? What would I do? Forget what I knew? Everything that had happened? Stan had checked in earlier today, and I'd given him a brief update—except I left out the part about Hunter. I wasn't hiding or protecting him from anything, I reasoned: he'd done nothing wrong as far as I knew, and I didn't want to distract the focus from finding the girl's identity. At least that's what I kept telling myself whenever my conscience reared its ugly head.

The house was empty when I got home. Hunter had a cross-country meet over an hour away, so he'd be lucky if he was home by ten. The older he got, the more it was just me in the house alone, and I didn't like the feeling. It was a reminder of how close we were to him going off to college and not being here anymore. I texted him good luck and headed to the kitchen to make tea, grateful I didn't have to make dinner for anyone but myself tonight. Just then my phone buzzed with a call, but it wasn't Hunter—it was her. It still startled me every time.

FELICIA: Hey! I was just thinking about you. I've been thinking about you all day.

CHLOE: I went to school today.

FELICIA: You did? How was it?

CHLOE: Awful.

FELICIA: Oh, no. Do you want to talk about it?

CHLOE: Everyone was staring at me and laughing at me. Everyone's seen the video. I spent all of free period hiding in the bathroom. I don't think I can go back.

FELICIA: I'm so sorry. That must've been terrible. Have you . . . have you actually seen the video yourself? Do you know what's on it?

CHLOE: Yeah, I've seen it. Someone snapped it to me a couple days ago. I've seen it so many times now, I couldn't even tell you how many. I keep watching. It's like I can't stop.

FELICIA: What's on it?

CHLOE: I'm running around naked, trying to find my clothes. I fall off the bed at the beginning. And I sort of remember that. Because it felt like my arms and my legs wouldn't work right, like I told you before? I was all floppy. My brain kept telling me to do different things, but I couldn't move. Then I charge at the person filming. That's when everyone laughs.

FELICIA: Do you recognize any of the boys?

CHLOE: No, of course not. They're not dumb. They don't show their faces, and they barely talk. They just laugh. That's what I remember the most. How they laughed. [deep sigh, resigned] I can't do this. I'm not going back. Everyone hates me and wishes I were dead. I might as well do them a favor.

FELICIA: That's not true! I understand how it must feel that way right now, but everybody *doesn't* hate you. There are people in your life that love you so much. Can we come up with a list of people that love you? And maybe we could pick one of those people to talk to? You might feel better if you let someone in your life know how you were feeling, so they could help you.

CHLOE: There's no help. Nothing's going to make this better.

FELICIA: But you won't know if you don't try.

CHLOE: Did you really feel like this? Like your life was over?

FELICIA: Yes, I did. I promise you. I know what it's like to be so afraid you can't sleep at night, and you can't stop thinking about what happened even when you want to. How little sounds scare you. Remember how I told you that I slept in my closet for two months after it happened?

CHLOE: That's right . . . I'm sorry.

FELICIA: Thank you. But I was so lucky to have people who held me up. My mom, my sisters, my friends. I couldn't do it alone. You're not going to be able to do it alone either. [pause] Is there anyone you can talk to that can help you? I know you're scared to tell your parents, but I bet they love you more than anything in the world.

CHLOE: They're going to be so disappointed in me. I just wanna die. I don't want to be here anymore.

FELICIA: [unsteady] Okay . . . How about this? The option to end things is always going to be there, right?

CHLOE: [hesitantly] Yes?

FELICIA: So, here's what I'm thinking. Why don't you give your parents a *chance* to help you first? Let them know what happened to you, and give them an opportunity to be there for you. Just try. See if it makes you feel any better. What do you have to lose at this point? If it doesn't work, and you still feel the same way, then we can talk about other options. Figure out what you want to do next. But at least you tried.

CHLOE: You really think I should tell my parents?

FELICIA: Absolutely. I think you should at least give it a try. I know I keep saying this, but what do you have to lose?

[Long pause]

CHLOE: I'll think about it . . . maybe I will . . .

She hung up before I could say anything else. The powerlessness of the situation washed over me. How awful for her to go to school alongside the boys that had assaulted her. To have to be in the same building as her rapists. No wonder she was feeling so terrible. I wanted to get her out of there, but I couldn't do it on my own. She was going to have to tell somebody besides me. Someone who was actually a part of her life and could help her. I crossed my fingers like a superstitious kid blowing out birthday candles that she was telling her parents right now.

There was something profoundly unsettling about knowing there was a group of boys right here in town who were that cruel. How could Hunter have anything to do with that?

He wouldn't. He couldn't.

Was what she said about everyone seeing the video true? If that many people had seen it, wouldn't at least one person have told an adult or reported it to someone? And why hadn't Hunter seen it? He seemed to know about all of the social drama, but I hadn't been through his phone since that first night. What if he had one of those burner apps Stan told me about? What if all his friends did? Was Hunter hiding a secret life from me the same way this poor girl was hiding this from her parents?

There was only one way to find out.

CHAPTER TEN

I walked into Hunter's room and was immediately flooded with guilt over what I was about to do. I never snooped through his stuff. I respected his boundaries and his space. My mother was terrible about going through my things when I was growing up— there was absolutely no privacy or boundaries in my house. She read my journal in seventh grade, and I felt so violated that I never kept another journal. I vowed never to be that way when I had my own kids, and I'd stuck to it, so being in here felt inherently wrong. But given the circumstances, I knew it was something I had to do. My mind wouldn't let me rest until I'd looked.

It'd been over an hour since I got off the phone with the girl, and I just kept wondering what was going on with her. Her situation consumed my thoughts. Had she listened to me? Did she decide to tell her parents? Was she talking to them right now? I kept trying to send her positive and supportive energy through some kind of mental telepathy. I really hoped she told them. Would I hear from her afterward? Probably not. If she had her parents and people around her that cared about her, there wouldn't be a need for me anymore. I already felt some of the weight leaving me with the possibility of not carrying the load. But I wasn't out of the woods yet.

I took a quick scan of Hunter's room, smiling at the tidy space. Unlike most teenagers, whose rooms looked like war zones, Hunter was neat and organized. He was meticulous about keeping his room clean, and it was a trait he'd inherited from me. I'd always used cleaning as a way of managing my anxiety. Something about straightening my environment helped me organize my thoughts. We were alike in so many ways.

His bed was done up and nicely made. His stuffed animals in a pullout drawer underneath it. His bookshelf was full of anime and other comic books. One of my proudest accomplishments as a mom was that I'd raised a reader. Our Barnes & Noble day trips were some of my fondest memories. The walls were decorated with posters of his favorite bands. Ones I'd never heard of before, with names like Blackpink and Glass Animals.

I stood in the middle of the room with my hands on my hips, anxiously going around in circles. I didn't even know what I was looking for, but after my conversation with the girl, I'd felt compelled to come in here and search. I'd gotten her to agree to tell her parents, and I didn't feel like I could rest until I'd done everything I could to settle matters with Hunter. Even if the two things were disconnected, he'd still lied to me about staying over at Shai's that night. He'd never lied to me before, and nobody lied without a reason.

I lifted up the mattress to see if he'd tucked anything underneath it, since that was one of my favorite hiding spots when I was a teenager. There was nothing. I moved to his nightstand and rifled through the drawer. It was practically empty except for a box of condoms and gum wrappers. I walked over to his dresser and pulled out each drawer, rifling through them one by one, being careful not to mess up his folded and color-coded clothes. I came up empty-handed there, too.

There was nothing out of the ordinary in his room. No clues. But that didn't make me feel any better. What I really needed was to get into his phone again. I'd only skimmed things the other morning when I was looking for the video. I hadn't delved into anything deeply, hadn't looked for any hidden apps. How was it possible that had only been two nights ago?

I walked over to his closet and opened the door. This was his only messy place: out of sight and out of mind. It reminded me of Monica's hallway closet on *Friends*. His backpacks and shoes cluttered the floor, you couldn't even see the carpet. The kid had so many shoes it was ridiculous. Clothes were stuffed everywhere, especially in the back. He was really good about doing all of his chores except laundry: he'd wait until he was on his last pair of clean socks before he did it. I'd stopped doing his clothes for him a few years back—in addition to needing his help around the house, I wasn't raising a man who expected people to take care of him. He was going to be a man that carried his load of household responsibilities if I had anything to do with it.

I rifled through all the stuff, cleaning and organizing as I went. I hung his backpacks on their hooks. Put his shoes in their places. He wouldn't be mad about me being in his room if I was helping out by cleaning the closet, right? Dirty clothes were mixed in with the clean ones, and I separated them, cringing when I grabbed a pair of his ex-girlfriend's tiny white underwear. I hurriedly tossed them in the hamper with the other dirty clothes. I'd always wondered if they were having sex, but I didn't need to wonder anymore. I hoped he used the condoms in the drawer. There was a shoebox I didn't recognize next to his red Jordans and I was surprised to discover it held all the sentimental things from their relationship—all the monthly anniversary cards she sent him, her favorite T-shirt, the teddy bear she gave him after he got his wisdom teeth pulled, and their formal Christmas pictures she'd forced him to get done. I shook my head. He told me he'd given her back all her stuff and thrown everything else out. He swore their breakup didn't bother him, but maybe he was just embarrassed to admit that he was missing her and hurting over it. Could Marissa have something to do with this?

They'd only been together for five months, but it seemed like an intense five months. The two of them had been practically inseparable, to the point where he started neglecting hanging out with his other friends, and even studying less. I was afraid she was one of those girls who'd attach themselves to a Division 1 athlete, since that's where he was headed, except he wouldn't be going anywhere if he let a relationship derail his focus. But just when I started getting worried and toying with the idea of approaching him about it, they abruptly broke up. I overheard a few screaming matches over FaceTime, and then nothing. He'd said she was done and gone, that he was over it. He'd even said having a girlfriend in high school was stupid, and I'd agreed.

Was she the girl he and Shai fought about? I hung up the last few jackets, then grabbed the basket to take downstairs to the laundry room and shut the door. I took one last glance at his room behind me.

Everything was in its place. You couldn't tell I'd even been in there except for the organized closet, which now matched the rest of the room. I rested my hand on the doorknob. Maybe it was finally over. The girl was going to tell her parents, and it was just a weird coincidence that Hunter was at the same party. It seemed like he could be lying to me about his ex-girlfriend, so he might've been equally embarrassed about whatever happened that night. Maybe I'd done all I could for both of them, and it was time to finally let it go, like Stan suggested. Get back to my own life again. I shut the door behind me, feeling peaceful for the first time in three days. I thought about taking a break from the call center until I regained my bearings. This had all been so much to process, and I might need some time to find normal again. But my peace of mind didn't last for long.

CHAPTER ELEVEN

Turn on Sky News right now!!! Stan texted me just as I was getting ready to leave for the office after working from home most of the morning. I headed right back inside the house, hurrying to the living room. I turned on the TV above the mantel and pulled up the guide to find the channel, since I rarely watched the local news.

Miguel and Rachel had been doing the morning show for the last twenty years. Hunter and I made fun of their bad plastic surgery on the rare occasions when we did watch. Rural Wisconsin didn't have the best plastic surgeons, and I always told him I'd go somewhere else to get work done if I were them. They looked like cartoon characters with their shiny, botoxed foreheads and ridiculously plump lips. Eyebrows off-kilter and crooked. This morning they were joking around, bantering back and forth as they returned from the commercial break. The camera focused in on them while they got ready to introduce the next segment.

"And now, for our next story," Rachel said, turning to Miguel. "Why don't you tell everyone what we have next?"

Miguel nodded enthusiastically, then his face turned serious. "The Danes say a terrible assault occurred three weeks ago when their freshman daughter was at a local party. The assailants recorded a video of the girl that's now being passed around school.

The parents are asking for your help in identifying the people involved in the attack, and bringing their daughter justice. They're here with us today to talk about the incident, and they're asking for anyone with information about the video or the party where it was recorded to come forward."

I froze in front of the TV. Everything stilled. I could barely swallow. It'd been two days since I'd heard from the girl—I'd replied to our last text chain a couple times to see how she was doing, and if she'd told her parents, but she hadn't responded. I'd taken it as "no news is good news" and hoped she didn't need me anymore because they were helping her. That was the point in making her tell them, and I thought it had worked. This was all supposed to be over.

A separate window with a video popped up on the TV screen. Mr. and Mrs. Danes sat together on a sofa in what I assumed was their living room. Mrs. Danes looked distraught. Her eyes were red and puffy. She'd probably been crying since she found out. Mr. Danes looked angry. She leaned into him for support, and he sat tall like a stiff board. His lips were pressed in a straight line. A vein throbbed in his jaw while he anxiously worked it, desperately trying to keep it together.

"Mr. and Mrs. Danes, thank you so much for being here today. I know this must be incredibly hard for you," Rachel opened. "Can you tell us a little bit more about what happened to your daughter?"

"Absolutely." Mr. Danes stared directly into the camera. His deep brown eyes seared into the audience. "The community needs to know we have predators in our midst. Our daughter, Chloe, came to us a few nights ago and let us know she'd been raped and assaulted by a group of boys while she was at a party." He spoke like even the words tasted bad. Like he was spitting them out.

"This is TV, and there might be children watching, so I'll spare you the details, but they brutalized my daughter. The things they did to her . . ." His voice cracked. Mrs. Danes gripped his hand while he struggled to gain control of his emotions. "And as if that wasn't enough, those monsters recorded her. They made a video, and it's been circulating on social media for almost a week."

Miguel's and Rachel's faces filled with concern. Both of them were parents, too. Miguel spoke first. "Before we go any further, I just want to say I'm so sorry that happened to your daughter. She—"

"Chloe." Mr. Danes interrupted him and stared into the camera. "Her name is Chloe. She's not just some anonymous girl in a video that you can trash-talk online. She's a real girl with hopes and dreams. One that has parents and siblings that love her. Who plays volleyball and runs track in the spring. She's an innocent little girl, and she has a name." He reached beside him and grabbed something—a framed photo—that he held up to the camera for all of us to see. "This is Chloe. You see her?" He leaned over and shoved the picture even closer to the camera, pointing to it with his other hand. "That's who she is. She's a real person, you monsters."

I didn't know her name. Her identity. She'd been just this anonymous voice on the phone. And then suddenly, there she was, right in front of my face. They used one of her school photos from Buckley, and I recognized the navy blue polo shirt with the white letters. The same one Hunter donned every day. I'd helped him find a clean one this morning. She was young—really young. Hazel eyes sparkling with light. Her smile was wide, exposing a set of braces like any other ninth grader's. A dash of freckles sprinkled across her nose. A tiny mole on her cheek underneath her eye.

Chloe Danes.

That was her name. Having a name and a face made it so much more personal.

Miguel and Rachel were both caught off guard, too. Neither of them had expected the photo. That ripped Chloe's anonymity wide open, and she was a minor. Had she given her consent to this interview? Did she know it was happening? My thoughts tumbled over each other, trying to make sense of it all.

"We've spent lots of time discussing the dehumanization and bullying that happens on social media, especially among young people. What is it you'd like to say to people today?" Rachel asked, quickly recovering from the shock of the unexpected photo—it was live TV, she had no other choice. She couldn't just end the interview.

"First, stop sharing the video and stop watching it. Please. You're no better than the monsters who recorded it, and you're breaking the law since she's a minor. All you're doing by watching that trash is further victimizing her. Stop." Mrs. Danes started silently weeping next to her husband. She buried her face in his shoulder while she cried. I could feel her pain through the screen. "Our daughter was drugged while attending a party at a local student's house, and we're going after everyone involved. The parents who hosted the party. The people that gave her the drugs. Whoever sold the drugs to those guys in the first place. We're going to find every single person involved in hurting our daughter, and we're going to make sure there are serious consequences for what they did to her."

"Has an official report been filed with the police?" Rachel asked.

"Of course. It's the first thing we did once we found out, and the police are working hand in hand with us to bring those monsters to justice. This is what happens when you let grown men attend high school. They were *men* that attacked my daughter." Mr. Danes furiously shook his head.

Rachel raised her eyebrows. "I'm sorry, but I'm not sure I'm following you."

The more he talked, the angrier he got, while his wife curled more and more into herself like she wanted to disappear from the entire moment. "It was an upperclassman party that she got invited to. Do you know how many seniors at Buckley are actually nineteen and even twenty years old? You let your boys be held back so they can play sports and develop advantages, then put them in class with children? We're going after every single one of them."

"Are you saying that she knew her attackers? They were her classmates?"

Mr. Dane shook his head. "Like I said, she was drugged, so she's having a difficult time identifying who they were, but I know those boys were there. It's why we didn't allow her to go to the party in the first place. It's why we keep her away from all that. Our young girls should not have to go to school with grown men."

Miguel quickly rattled off the statistics of how common it'd become, especially within the last five years, to hold boys back in kindergarten and again in middle school. By the time they got to high school, they were a full two years older than the rest of the students in their class. He talked about how there were two nineteen-year-olds at Buckley and one twenty-year-old—two were basketball players and the other a football player. I knew it happened, but Hunter was a runner, and that sort of thing didn't happen in his sport. The last thing you wanted in a runner was for them to be too big. Size gave no advantage. So I never thought much about this practice or its implications.

"If we find out that one of them was involved, we're suing the school. Because guess what? There's a reason we don't let our teenage daughter hang out with men, especially around men drinking alcohol."

"You've come here today to ask for the community's support. What can we do to help you?" Rachel asked. Her eyes were kind.

"The investigators have created an anonymous tip line for anyone with information about that night, or the drugs, or the video to come forward." The number flashed on the bottom of the screen.

Mrs. Danes finally lifted her head from her husband's shoulder and pulled away from him. She gave her first look at the camera. The devastation in her eyes rocked me to my core. The unrelenting pain of a mother who'd discovered her child had been hurt. We felt it in our bodies, like it was happening to us.

"Please . . . please . . ." Her voice warbled. She was doing everything she could do not to burst into tears while she spoke. "They hurt my baby girl so bad, and you've got to help us find who did this to her. Please."

Rachel's eyes filled with tears. She had three girls of her own. One of them was a junior at Buckley. "I'm so sorry this is happening, and we wish you and your family all the love and support possible while you go through this difficult time." Rachel shifted her gaze to the camera, to everyone watching. The tip line number flashed back on the screen. "The number to call is at the bottom of your screen, and we're asking all of you to help find Chloe's attackers and bring them to justice. If you can think of any information that might be helpful, reach out. Talk to your kids. See what they know. And please, don't share the video."

Mr. and Mrs. Danes gripped each other tightly. "Thanks, Rachel."

Miguel's and Rachel's faces were grim as the video box of the Danes disappeared.

"Wow," Miguel said solemnly. "What a terrible tragedy. I hope our viewers are able to help."

"Yes, me too," Rachel agreed, nodding her head. "I think we might need a break after all that, and when we come back, maybe we can show clips from last night's puppy show at the 4H building? Feel like we all need something to help us feel better."

"Definitely," Miguel said, turning around to face the camera. "We'll be back soon with the Winston Dog Festival."

They cut to commercial. I sat in front of the TV while my brain swirled. When I said she should go to her parents, I'd never expected her parents to go to the media. I wasn't prepared to see a victim's face, especially a child's, broadcast on live TV like that. And I wasn't sure how I felt about it. All I could think about was Hunter and how private he was. He didn't even like me posting anything about him on social media to my small handful of friends and followers. I used to post all the time: cute photos of us out and about around town, or celebrating holidays. But once he hit middle school, he started getting embarrassed by it, so I only posted stuff he gave me permission to.

Chloe— I paused. That was her name. It felt strange to think of her with a name. And now a face. Because Mr. Danes had plastered it all over the screen. Was he supposed to do that? I'd seen Rachel's and Miguel's expressions when he did. They'd both looked totally surprised, then quickly brushed it off, but I'd caught it. Didn't we try to keep victims' information private? Especially when they were minors?

I just couldn't imagine Chloe wanted this. She'd been so secretive. And mortified. Her father had brought up the video and asked people not to watch it, but that seemed like wishful thinking to me. Telling people there was a video out there probably just piqued their curiosity, and they could be googling it right now.

What had I done?

CHAPTER TWELVE

"How did you know this was happening? Did they go to the police? Were you the one to take the statement? How did Chloe seem?" I questioned Stan rapid fire, barely able to catch my breath. I'd called him as soon as I got in my car, hoping he was one of the detectives that met with the Danes down at the station.

"They came in yesterday morning, and it was an absolute disaster. We already knew we needed everybody ready and all hands on deck because Mr. Danes called the night before, and he was absolutely furious. Understandable, but he was ready to go find those boys and take care of them himself, so we had to try to de-escalate the situation."

That detail stopped me in my tracks. I knew there was a gun in the house somewhere. Did Stan remember that? Of course he did. He'd be a terrible detective if he didn't. "Was Chloe with him?"

"She was."

"What was she like?" He could lose his job for having this conversation with me, and I could hear the slight hesitation in his voice. But he knew me well enough to know he could trust me. Also, I'd helped him navigate the sticky gray edges of his divorce a few years back, free of charge, and he owed me a favor.

"I didn't take her statement, but she wasn't in a good place at all, and I'm pretty sure she wasn't there willingly. Her and her mom both seemed a bit shell-shocked, but Mr. Danes had shifted into take-down mode. He was determined to go after everyone involved, and nothing was going to stop him. Honestly, I'd feel the same way. Who wouldn't? He bulldozed his way into the station and forced her down there, too, but what other choice did he have? You couldn't *not* report something like that. If there are high school kids going around drugging girls at parties and assaulting them, you've got to do whatever you can to stop it. And . . . listen, I didn't tell you this until now because I don't work sex crimes and hadn't talked with them about the case until yesterday, but there've actually been a few other instances of young girls being drugged and raped within the last year. The detectives investigating those cases are wondering if Chloe's is related, so it's an even more serious issue than we originally thought. Not that it wasn't serious to begin with." He cleared his throat. "Anyway, we called in our crisis response team and one of our victim advocates is the one who took her statement."

"But forcing her to go down to the police station and give a statement before she was ready . . . don't you think it could all backfire?" I realized the hypocrisy in what I'd just said. *I* was the one who made her tell her parents before she was ready. And look what happened.

"I know. Feels harsh, but he wasn't wrong. It's now been weeks since the assault, and we've already lost valuable time. All the physical evidence is gone. Washed away. Now our team is working its way backward. We're going through the video, and a few of the officers are headed out to the school today to question students."

I wondered if Chloe was at school today. How was she supposed to go to school after something like this? Before, I'd told her there was no way everybody knew about what happened, but this changed everything. If there was a remote chance somebody didn't know about the assault or the video as of yesterday, it was gone now.

"Did she say who did it?" I asked. Maybe that would be the saving grace in all of this. They'd arrest the boys who hurt her and she could start to heal.

This time there was even more hesitation to answer my question. "We're compiling a list of names of possible suspects," Stan said, being intentionally vague.

I didn't push. I wanted to keep him on my side. But I was dying to know if Hunter was on the list. Or what about Shai? Any of his other friends? "Have you watched the video?" I asked instead.

"I have." His voice grew thick with emotion. No doubt he was thinking about his ten-year-old daughter at home. Only a few years younger than Chloe.

"And?"

"It's awful. Like, really awful. There's nothing of the actual assault, but they start filming her afterward, when she's super disoriented and traumatized. You can tell she's terrified and has no idea what's happening." He paused for a second, clearly wrestling with his emotions. "You want to know the worst part about the whole thing?"

I couldn't imagine the worst part. It all seemed awful, and I hadn't even seen it. I didn't think I ever would. I wasn't sure I wanted to live with those disturbing images in my head. Hearing about it had already been too much.

"It's the laughing. The way they're all mocking her and making fun of her, especially this one guy. It's the cruelest thing I've ever seen, and it's burned into my soul in a way I'm never going to forget. Makes me question what the hell is wrong with kids these days. How could anyone do that? How do you take enjoyment in another person's suffering and humiliation like that?"

I just shook my head. I didn't know either. It was impossible not to be affected by her case. "I just don't know what I'm supposed to do now. I haven't heard anything from her since this all came out. All I can think about is how she's doing, especially after all this attention. Did she even know her parents were going to go on the morning show? How did that even happen?"

"Mr. Danes is one of the executives at the station. I don't think they could say no to him. I watched it, too, and you could tell Miguel and Rachel were shocked when he held up her picture. I understand why he feels like this is necessary, but I'm not sure it's the best move. He has a very clear idea of what needs to be done and exactly how it has to happen, though. And he doesn't seem like a man who's used to being told no or not getting his way."

"I just don't know what to do," I repeated myself. I'd been parked in the lot in front of my office for the last few minutes. I didn't know how I could shut all these emotions off and just go do my job. Especially now that I had a name and face. All I kept seeing was the picture Chloe's father had flashed. Her smile. The navy-blue Buckley polo. Something about her being in uniform was like an extra stab to the heart.

"There's nothing you can do, Felicia. You're just going to have to do your best to let it go. Let the people who are trained to deal with these sorts of things be the ones to handle it."

Maybe he was right. I'd already done enough damage. The more I tried to help fix things, the worse they got. Maybe I should just step out of the way and let them take care of it. But deep down, I knew I was partially responsible for today. I was the one who'd made her go to her parents. This was probably why she was so afraid of her dad.

"Okay," I said. "Just don't forget, there's a gun in the house."

CHAPTER THIRTEEN

"Do you need to take that?" my client asked with a slight eye roll. Usually, I turn my phone on silent and tuck it away during any meeting with clients—it was inconsiderate to have it on the table. But today, I couldn't take the chance of missing a call from Chloe. So far, she hadn't called, but lots of other people had. The phone had been vibrating through our entire meeting.

"I'm sorry," I said. "I know it's rude to have my phone out, but I'm waiting on a really important call. I can't miss it." I'd already explained that to her before we sat down.

She raised her eyebrows as if to say: Wasn't she important? She really was the worst client to be doing this with, because she already required delicate handling. One of those people who thought the world revolved around them, and everyone else was just a pawn in their universe. If I'm being honest, it didn't surprise me that her husband was divorcing her.

"Maybe you'd like to reschedule?" She said it so snottily, and any other day, I would've been able to ignore it and push through. I dealt with difficult and hostile people all the time, it came with the job. But today, I didn't have it in me.

"You know what?" I asked, starting to gather all of her financial disclosures, which I'd laid out on the table for us to go over. "That's probably a good idea. Let's just reschedule this meeting."

Her jaw dropped, and she was clearly annoyed. She'd said it, but she hadn't really meant it. She was only trying to make a point, but now it was too late. Maybe next time she wouldn't be so passive-aggressive.

I tucked all the papers into their respective folders and quickly slid them inside my briefcase. "Why don't you call my assistant and have her book a new time for us?"

She huffed, insulted, but I didn't care. I turned around and headed out of the conference room before she had a chance to say anything else. Let her find different counsel if she wanted to. It wasn't like I didn't have a wait list of clients who would be more than happy to fill her spot.

I headed down the hallway toward my office but, at the last minute, took a turn and hopped on the elevator instead. I couldn't be here today. I'd cleared my entire afternoon for this client, so now it was free, and I couldn't spend it working. I didn't know where I was going, but I had to get out of there and clear my head.

I took the elevator down to the parking garage and decided to head to Saul's for lunch. There was nothing like comfort food to make you feel better, and an order of pancakes slathered in their homemade syrup might be exactly what I needed.

The server recognized me immediately and brought me to my favorite table. I'd been coming here for breakfast since before I had Hunter. Breakfast food was my favorite, and I was always one of those people who believed it was perfectly acceptable to eat it for any meal—lunch or dinner. Hunter was the same way. This was his favorite place, too. We used to come here on Saturday mornings after his swimming lessons.

Thoughts of Hunter got me running through the conversation I was going to have with him when he got home tonight. Now that the assault had been blown wide open and everyone knew about it, I didn't have to pretend like I didn't. I could have an actual conversation about what happened without being so secretive.

Was he one of the kids on the list to be interviewed today? I couldn't imagine the ensuing shitstorm when parents found out the police were interviewing their kids at school without their consent. Parents always thought police needed their permission to talk to their kids, but technically, they didn't. I wondered how they were going to figure out who was at the party. Or were they just interviewing the entire school? I had so many questions, but I knew I'd definitely exceeded my limit with Stan. He'd already given me more than he was supposed to, and I didn't want to push it.

I felt much better after a good meal followed by a nap in my favorite chair in the living room. I took a nice long shower when I woke up, and by the time Hunter got home from practice, I was refreshed, clearheaded, and ready for our conversation.

"Hey, hon," I called out when I heard him at the front door. "Can you come into the living room? I want to talk to you about something."

His footsteps padded through the house. "What's up?" he asked, taking a seat across from me on the leather chair. He plopped his feet on the ottoman. His forehead shone with sweat and his hair stuck up all over the place. It was always wild after his practices.

"I wanted to talk to you about Jett's party again," I said slowly, gauging his face for a reaction. Instant annoyance. Then, a dramatic eye roll.

"Mom, good lord, we already talked about it. How many times are you going to ask me the same question? It wasn't even a big deal. I told you—me and Shai are fine. We worked it out. You worry too damn much," he said, giving me a dimpled smile at the joke we'd had since he was ten.

It was funny, because the first time he said it was also the first time he'd ever sworn at me or in front of me. One of those milestones you didn't know was happening until after it was over. He was in fifth grade and getting ready to go on his first overnight sleepover at the wilderness adventure club outside of Madison. He was fine, but I was a nervous wreck, scurrying around the house and snapping at him about everything he needed to pack until he finally reached his limit and snapped back.

He froze after he said it. Afraid he was going to get into trouble. It was one of the worst things he'd ever done—said a swear word. Big trouble in his mind, and he was a rule follower. But I'd just burst out laughing because of how strange it sounded coming out of his mouth and because he was right: I was being ridiculous. Relief had swept his face and he started laughing along with me. We'd been laughing about it ever since. "You worry too damn much" had become one of our favorite inside jokes.

"That's not what I wanted to talk to you about. I'm not worried about the fight, that's between you and Shai, I'm just glad it's resolved," I said. "I want to know what happened while you were at the party."

He raised his eyebrows. Tucked his hands into his hoodie. "What do you mean?"

I cocked my head to the side. Did he really not know what I was talking about? I asked directly. "Weren't the police at your school today?"

He balked. Hesitated. "The police were at my school?"

I nodded. "Yes. I heard they were interviewing kids about the party at Jett's."

A confused expression crossed his face along with something else—something I couldn't quite make sense of, but it quickly passed. "I didn't see any police on campus. I don't understand. What happened?"

"You haven't heard?" I probed his eyes, searching for clues, but I'd lost the ability to read them. He felt like a stranger in that moment. It made me dizzy. I scooted forward on the couch and planted my feet firmly on the ground like that would steady my insides. "A girl named Chloe Danes was assaulted at that party, and a group of boys recorded her afterward. She just went to the police and filed charges. Her dad is determined to find out who did it. I heard the police were at the school today, interviewing kids who were at the party. I figured since you were there, they might have interviewed you . . ."

"Who told you that?"

"Told me what? About the assault? It was on the news."

He scowled at me and shook his head. "No, that the police were at the school today."

That struck me as an odd question. What did it matter? "My friend Stan. We'd been talking about it."

"You talked about it before they went there? But how did you know?"

These weren't any of the questions I'd expected. Suddenly, I felt like I was being interrogated, and I didn't know why. "We met for drinks last weekend, and he mentioned something about it."

Hunter stared back at me like he was trying to decide whether or not he believed my story. I was a terrible liar, always had been, so the truth was probably written all over my face. But he didn't press any further. Was he angry? Why on earth was he reacting this way?

I gave him my most serious face. "Hunter, if you know anything about what happened to Chloe or the video, I need you to tell me."

"I don't know anything about what happened, but I can tell you this"—his scowl quickly faded into a cocky grin I'd never seen—"Chloe really likes to party."

"You know her?" I asked, trying to pretend I wasn't horrified by his response.

He snorted. "Of course I know Chloe. Everyone does. She's one of *those* girls."

"Hunter!"

"Sorry, Mom, but she is. Chloe is always partying. She's all over that scene. And the other thing about Chloe you probably don't know? She loves attention. You should see her Instagram. Go look at it. You'll see exactly what I'm talking about. Honestly, I wouldn't be surprised if she made this entire thing up for attention, to get everyone talking about her."

I wanted to slap the words out of his mouth. I remembered our first conversation—how young and lost she sounded, explaining that she didn't even drink. I spoke through gritted teeth, "Even if she *likes to party,* that doesn't mean she deserved for such a horrible thing to happen to her. I can't believe you'd say something like that. Have some compassion!"

He casually shrugged his shoulders like it wasn't a big deal, but I was horrified. "I'm sorry, Mom, but it is what it is. You have no idea what girls are like these days. They'll do anything for attention. And the video? She's probably the one that posted it."

"Are you serious right now?" I shook my head. I was disgusted with him, and I'd never been disgusted with him before. "I can tell you this—there is absolutely no way she posted that video of herself. It's degrading and awful."

"You've seen the video? How'd you see the video?"

"I didn't, but there was a piece about it on the news this morning, and that's what her dad said."

"The news?"

"Yes, Chloe's dad went on the morning show to ask for help in finding her attackers. They've created a tip line and a reward for anyone that provides information leading to their arrest."

He rolled his eyes.

"Hunter," I admonished again. "Don't act like that. This is very serious. A crime has been committed."

He pushed the ottoman away and stood. Jutted his hip out while he adjusted his backpack. "Are we done now? I'm super smelly, and I really need a shower."

I stared at him, trying to reconcile his response with the kind, compassionate son I'd always known. The one I'd raised to respect women. To treat them with dignity, and as equals. "So, to be clear, you don't know anything about what happened at the party or the video?"

"God, Mom, no, I already told you that," he said, turning his back to me and heading up the stairs. He stopped right before he got to the top. "Please stop asking me about it, too. I'm over this conversation."

CHAPTER FOURTEEN

It was another sleepless night as I tossed and turned in my bed. I spent all evening watching Hunter like he was a strange guest in my home. Shortly after our confrontation, I was cutting the pizza I'd just taken out of the oven when he came up behind me in the kitchen and changed the entire energy in the room. I felt him before he even got close to me. And not in a good way. The hairs on my neck bristled as he stood behind me.

"Raven and Talia are coming over in like ten minutes to give me their biology notes, since I missed class for that dentist appointment last week. That cool?" he asked.

"Sure," I said in the weird high-pitched voice I'd been using ever since our conversation about Chloe. I held my breath. Clutched the knife to keep my hand from shaking. Gripped the pot holder with the other hand. I couldn't turn around. *Please go away*, I thought. *Just go away.*

And then suddenly, he poked me in my ribs, and I jumped, banging my hip on the counter and dropping the knife on the floor. My body felt hot like I had a fever. His presence was making me sick.

"Oh my god, Mom." He laughed. "I totally got you that time." He gave me a teasing push and a big cheesy grin before grabbing a plate and piling it with pizza.

I was on edge the rest of the night. Every sound made me jump. How could he say those things about Chloe? There wasn't an ounce of concern or compassion in his voice. And he'd just carried on as if it wasn't a big deal. He laughed and fooled around with Raven and Talia like our conversation never even happened.

After his friends left, he hung out in the family room playing video games like it was just a regular Friday night. Most of the time, he did his thing, and I did mine. We were so comfortable coexisting we barely noticed each other. But not tonight.

I sat in my office listening and watching him while I pretended to work. I paid close attention to the way he talked in his headset to the people he was gaming with. Calling them trash. Telling them they sucked. Letting out squeals when he earned kills.

"Head shot, bitch!" He must've said it ten times. I cringed.

And I just kept cringing at the things coming out of his mouth. It was so shocking to all us moms when the kids started playing video games, especially first-person shooter games. The way they interacted and treated each other was horrible, but they all did it, so none of us thought to stop it. Maybe we should have. The violent video game behavior had become so commonplace over the years, I didn't even notice it anymore, but tonight I did. Tonight, it scared me.

There had been real hate and disgust in his tone when he talked about Chloe, which seemed like it applied to all women. He didn't say she deserved what happened to her, but he might as well have. It made me question everything about him, and all my fears rose to the surface. All this time that I'd been worried and concerned about him and what happened that night, I couldn't really imagine he was in that room with Chloe.

My real fear at the start was that he knew what happened and said nothing. That he let those boys hurt her and didn't do anything to stop them. Or that Shai had been involved, and he was covering for his friend. Part of me thought that's what their issue had been. Maybe she was the girl they were fighting over because Shai had been one of the boys to attack her. I'd never seen Shai show the slightest inkling of violence, but it was easier to consider being wrong about him than it was to consider being wrong about my own son.

What if he was in the room when it happened? What if he was one of the voices laughing and mocking her on the video? It was like I'd unconsciously blocked my brain from going there, but now, there was no going back. And as much as I didn't want to admit it, I was terrified at the possibility my son was involved in assaulting an innocent girl.

I didn't know what to do with the feelings. I'd never felt so powerless or disoriented in my own home. When he gave me a hug before he went up to his bedroom for the night, I actually flinched. It was just a second, but my body involuntarily reacted that way. What did it mean? My head swirled with so many questions. My emotions were just as confused.

By then, I was exhausted. This had to be a weird PTSD response. I'd been so stressed for the past week, and he was reminding me of his dad. That was all. Just because all that had been triggered didn't mean there was truth to it. I knew enough about PTSD to know it wasn't always grounded in fact. Maybe my mind was playing tricks on me. I was going to call my therapist in the morning. I hadn't seen her in a few years, but I couldn't stand looking at Hunter the way I was a second longer. When I'd shut my bedroom door tonight, I considered locking it. That's when I knew I was being absurd.

Hunter was a good boy. He was. All of this was just stirring up old memories. I couldn't bring my own experience into this moment with my son—it wasn't fair to him.

My phone buzzed on the nightstand next to my bed and I

rolled over to grab it. Another unknown number, but it had to be Chloe. I answered immediately.

This time was completely different. I knew exactly who she was. I knew what she looked like, and I could drive to her house if I needed to. All I had to do was look her up. And then it dawned on me that's all anyone else had to do either. She was completely exposed to the world. And if my own son had such a terrible reaction to her, and he was supposed to be one of the good guys, then what had other responses been?

She was crying hysterically on the other end of the phone, just like she'd been the night she called the center. I said the same things:

FELICIA: I'm here. I'm on the line. You're okay. You're not alone.

CHLOE: He-he-he . . . He– [sobbing too hard to speak]

FELICIA: It's okay. It's okay. Just let it out.

CHLOE: [shrieking voice] They texted me tonight. They texted me!

FELICIA: Who?

CHLOE: They did! I don't know which one, but I know it was them. One of them. I've been getting messages all day long. Texts and DMs. Do you know what people are saying to me? Saying to my family? The stuff they're sending my sister? [sobbing hard in between words] Do you know how many people said I should just die? That I should kill myself? Do you have any idea? And then there's my favorite: "You can't rape the willing."

FELICIA: Oh my god . . . I'm so sorry.

CHLOE: Don't tell me you're sorry! You did this! You told me to tell my parents. That's what you said– [mocking tone] *Oh, they'll help you. You'll see, it'll make you feel better.* Do you have any idea what my dad wants to do? Do you?

FELICIA: I saw your parents on the news today.

CHLOE: You saw them? [gulping for air like she's trying to stop crying]

FELICIA: [softly] I did.

CHLOE: So you know all about it, then. But you know what else he did? He created an Instagram profile, @JusticeForChloe. And he wants me to make a video for it. That's all he kept doing tonight. [mimicking his deep voice] *C'mon, Chloe, this is important. Come on, Chloe, we have to do this.* And he won't listen to me. He doesn't care. All he wants to do is find those boys, but you know what? I don't even care about those stupid boys anymore. I didn't want them to go to the media. I didn't want to tell anyone. Now the whole world knows. They never even asked me.

FELICIA: Chloe, I– Is it okay if I use your name?

CHLOE: I don't care. Nothing matters. This is all so unfair. My friend was there, too, but they only recorded me. And I'm not saying I wanted it to happen to her, too, but . . . She's not going to have to move. Change her whole life. [lets out a cry] Why me? Why did they just want to destroy my life? [sobbing too hard to continue]

FELICIA: None of this is fair, or your fault.

CHLOE: But none of that matters. Don't you see that? Everyone knows who I am. And no boy is ever gonna want to have anything to do with me. Who's gonna want to touch me when they know I'm trash? A disgusting piece–

FELICIA: Look, Chloe, stop. You are not trash. Do you hear me? There is absolutely nothing disgusting about you. You are a beautiful young woman who had something horrible happen to you, and I'm–I'm so sorry. And I'm sorry your parents didn't respect your wishes.

CHLOE: You told me they'd help me! You said if I told them that they would find a way to help me! Now it just made everything worse.

FELICIA: You're right—I didn't think that would happen, and I'm sorry. I just didn't want you to be alone. I never thought they'd make it so public.

CHLOE: What am I supposed to do now? I've gotta move. Go to a different school . . . This is all your fault. It's all your fault. You told me to tell them. You kept telling me, *Go to your parents, they'll help you.*

FELICIA: I know I did, and I really thought it was the best thing. I'm sorry. I didn't—

CHLOE: Stop saying you're fucking sorry! Oh my god, if you say it one more time, I swear to God, I don't know what I'm going to do.

FELICIA: Okay, okay, I'm— Let's try and figure this out together. What are we going to do?

CHLOE: What are *we* going to do? [disgruntled laugh] You're going to go on with your happy little life answering the phone for all the poor messed-up kids that call in. You're going to fill their heads full of bullshit just like you did to me. And then you'll be done, congratulating yourself for being such a great volunteer and giving back to the community. Like nothing ever happened.

FELICIA: That's not true. Really, Chloe, I haven't thought about anything else since you called in. I've barely slept. All I've done is wait to hear from you and try to figure out how I can help you.

CHLOE: Oh, please! You know why I really called tonight?

FELICIA: I think you called because you're really upset, and believe me, Chloe, you have every right to be upset. Angry with me. Angry with your dad. The police. The boys. All of it. I'd be so angry and upset if I were you.

CHLOE: Oh, that's not why I called. [snort-laughs] Remember what you said before? Your brilliant idea? *Tell your parents and if that doesn't make it better, then we can decide what to do next.* Well, I've already decided.

I tried reaching out to my parents just like you said, and it made things worse. So, I'm just calling to tell you goodbye. Because that's what you said—that I had a choice. So this is what I'm choosing. I don't want to be here anymore. I never should've listened to anything you said.

FELICIA: No, Chloe. You don't mean that. Honey, listen to me. I did not mean it that way. I didn't. Please don't do anything to hurt yourself. Please.

CHLOE: Well, I guess you shouldn't have said all that then, because I believed you. You want to hear something? [long pause. An audible click, then another, like a gun being cocked]

DISPATCHER: [cuts into call; Felicia has called 911 and added them to the call]: 911, what's your emergency?

FELICIA: [talking fast] My friend is on the line with us and I'm afraid she's going to hurt herself. Chloe, do you have a gun? Are you at home?

CHLOE: [laughs] Nice try. [dial tone, end of call]

FELICIA: Chloe! Chloe, did you hang up? Chloe? [dial tone fades out]

DISPATCHER: Ma'am, I'm still on the line. What's your location?

FELICIA: Ohmygod, please, you have to help her. Please, somebody help her!

DISPATCHER: Ma'am, what's your name?

FELICIA: My name? Who cares about my name—she's Chloe Danes. That's her name. Chloe Danes. And I know where she's calling from . . . I can give you the address. I just have to look it up. [rustling, movement, breathing hard] Here, 554 Thorn Road. You have to help her. Please, don't let her hurt herself! There's a gun in that house. She has a gun. I heard it. We have to stop her in time—

DISPATCHER: Help is on the way. We're doing everything we can.

CHAPTER FIFTEEN

At first glance, the psych ward seemed like a hospital floor that had been transformed into a college dorm. Tiny studio apartments with common spaces. Not at all like a regular hospital. Everyone, even most of the nurses and staff on the floor, wore regular clothes. There was no medical equipment. No machine sounds or beeping. So, it really felt like walking into a college dorm, until you looked a little closer. The world of no edges or sharp corners. Nobody had shoelaces or wore belts. Most of the furniture was bolted to the floor.

I walked slowly down the hallway. I'd never been in a psychiatric facility before. It'd been three days since Chloe was admitted. Her seventy-two-hour hold was officially over, but they were still keeping her. She'd probably be here for a while, but at least she was safe. From herself, from the boys who attacked her, from the kids at school still making her life hell. I'd called her parents as soon as I got off the phone with the 911 dispatcher, going straight to the school's directory and finding their number.

Chloe had barricaded herself in the bathroom with a gun, and it took two hours to get her out. I'd checked in with her dad every day since: He was incredibly grateful I'd gotten her to tell him, and even more grateful I called him and 911 that night. They'd agreed to put me on Chloe's visitor list, and she said she wanted to see me, too. But now that I was here, I had no idea what I was going to say to her.

I walked up to the nurses' station in the center of the floor. The one space resembling a traditional hospital setting.

"Excuse me, I'm here to see Chloe Danes?" I said to the woman furiously typing behind the huge desk. I never understood how people could type with acrylic nails, but she was a pro. Her fingernails clacked on the keys while she spoke.

"Are you on her visitor list?" she asked without looking up.

"I am."

She grabbed a clipboard lying next to her and slapped it on the desk. "Sign in. Then, just wait in room 22B over there on the left"—she briefly glanced up, motioning to the hallway behind her—"and someone will bring her to you shortly."

"Thanks," I said, scrawling my name at the bottom of the list.

Room 22B was tiny. Just two molded plastic chairs and a table. Empty beige walls matching the beige-carpeted floors. The color seemed a bit depressing for a psychiatric facility, but maybe it was calming. I had no idea.

I didn't have time to get any more nervous, because the door opened as soon as I sat down in the chair closest to the wall. Chloe was led in by one of the nurses. He dropped her off, then closed the door and posted himself up right outside the door. The head nurse had called yesterday to go over the visiting procedures, and she explained that Chloe was still on one-to-one supervision.

Before I knew what I was doing, I was out of my chair and wrapping my arms around her, squeezing her frail body tight against mine. I was halfway through the hug when I realized I'd thrown myself at her without asking her permission. I pulled back and held her at arm's length while I looked at her. Here. Alive. In front of me. "I'm sorry, I just . . . I'm so glad you're safe." Tears glistened in my eyes. I didn't realize I'd get so emotional seeing her. She looked slightly embarrassed, like any teenager. Her long hair was in a messy bun on top of her head. She wore flannel pajama bottoms and a big gray hoodie.

"It's okay," she said, stuffing her hands in her pockets and shuffling to the other chair. She curled into a ball in the chair, bringing her knees up to her chest. No shoes. Hospital grippy socks on her feet. She looked so different from the school picture they'd shown on TV. No makeup. So much younger. Still a child.

"Thanks for seeing me today." All I'd done for the last three days was think about all the things I wanted to say to her, but the words disappeared as soon as she was sitting in front of me. I just wanted to take her in my arms and let her cry. Had someone done that for her in here? That's what I wanted to ask. *Has someone held you?* But instead of unloading all my questions, I just sat in silence, waiting for her to lead the way this time. She'd ended up safe, but I couldn't help but feel like we all failed her.

Her eyes were heavy, like she was medicated or sleepy. It was hard to tell which, and I had nothing to compare it to.

"My mom just left. Did you see her?" she asked, finally breaking the silence.

"No." *Please let her have a good mama,* I thought. She'd looked wrecked on TV, but you never knew who people were behind closed doors. "Did you have a good . . . visit with her?" I didn't know what else to call it.

Her lower lip quivered. "She just read me Harry Potter like she used to do when I was little and got sick." The tension coiling my insides released. The weight of the full responsibility immediately lifted. "She's really mad at my dad, too. Like, making-him-sleep-in-the-guest-bedroom kind of mad. And that's only happened one other time in my whole life." A tear slipped down her cheek. She brushed it away with the back of her sleeve. "She hates that he made her go on TV." I hated that for her, too. Chloe glanced up at me, real eye contact for the first time. "I'm glad you made me tell my parents, though. Even if I did end up in here. I needed my mom."

I reached across the table and grabbed her hands, squeezing them tight and doing my best not to cry. "I'm so glad to hear you say that. Honestly, sweetie, I had no idea what I was doing. All I wanted to do was keep you safe and alive. I knew there were people out there that loved you, and I'm so glad your mama showed up for you. Sounds like your dad tried, too, in his way." I didn't want to forget about him or let him get thrown under the bus. His intentions were good. Same as mine.

"I know he did." Her body slowly melted in the chair. I felt so relieved not to have to ask about her mental health or her state of mind. She was in the hands of real professionals. People who knew how to help her. Ones who could keep her safe so I didn't have to anymore.

"I won't stay long because I know you have limited free time, and I don't want to take up all of it. I just wanted to come see you and let you know I'm here if you ever need anything. You have my number in your phone, obviously." I gave her a wink and she gave me a little smile back. She was going to be okay. Not right now, and probably not for a long time, but I could see that fighter spirit in her eyes. "Don't be afraid to reach out. I know everybody always says it, but I mean it." I gave her a pointed look and another smile. "And you know I'm the girl that always answers your calls, no matter what time it is."

"Oh, I know." She was still smiling. It looked beautiful on her face. "You're the only one I can talk to about what really happened, you know. I can't talk to the police." She shook her head. Her voice slowed. The light in her eyes was gone that quick. "They've been here a bunch of times, but I can't answer their questions. I just freeze. My mom's there with me, and she doesn't push me . . . That other lady is, too. The advocate or whatever they call her." She stared at the floor, anxiously twirling the hair that'd fallen in her face. "Can I tell you something?" She kept her gaze down.

"Of course. You can tell me anything."

"I can't talk about what happened with my mom there. I know she's there to support me and all that, but all the questions . . . the things they have to ask me. Like . . ." She dropped her voice to a whisper. "It's all the bad sexual stuff they want to ask me about. And it's all these in-depth questions about every detail, you know? Did they do that to you, too?"

I nodded. "They did, and it was awful. I hated every single minute. I'm sorry you have to go through it."

"But I *want* to tell my story. I really do. Even if it's awful. I want them to find those guys and punish them." She slowly lifted her gaze from the floor. Sadness filled her eyes. "My mom flinches next to me all the time . . . and she lets out these little whimpering sounds? I'm not sure she even knows she's doing it. She can't even handle their *questions,* so she definitely can't handle my answers and I don't want to hurt her. I—" And then she started crying.

"Oh, sweetie, it's going to be okay. Can I give you a hug?" She nodded and I hurried around the table, engulfing her in a huge hug, chair and all. If she thought this would hurt her mother, imagine what losing her forever would've felt like. But I didn't say that. It wasn't what she needed to hear. "This must be so hard for both of you."

She looked up at me. "Do you . . . do you think you could be there?"

"When you talk to the police, to give a statement?"

She nodded.

"As long as that's okay with the officers. I've never been in a situation like this, so I don't know what the protocol is, but I don't see why not. If you want me there, I'd certainly be there for you." The thought of it made me sick, but I'd do anything to help her.

Her face relaxed and she wiped her eyes. "Okay, I'll ask. Oh, and one more thing? Can you tell my mom all of that for me, too? I feel like you can explain it better. I don't want to hurt her feelings."

"Of course, sweetie. Anything you need." Maybe this would be the thing I could do to make it right by her, after everything I'd done wrong. To be there with her when she gave her statement and help her put away the boys who'd hurt her? It might make all of the pain worth it.

CHAPTER SIXTEEN

I sat next to Chloe, holding her hand as she went through the gruesome details of her attack with the detectives. It'd been over an hour but we were almost finished.

The conversation with Mrs. Danes beforehand had gone well. She grabbed my arm after I explained Chloe's feelings and her desire to have me sit in on the forensic interview, and she said, "Would you do that? Would you help her get through it?" Her eyes held trauma similar to Chloe's. Someone needed to find her a therapist, too. "It's just so hard for me to hear how they hurt her. I can barely stand it. I feel it in my bones. And the anger. I've never felt anything like it." She shuddered. Her jaws clenched automatically. "But I want to be there for her. I really do."

"How about this? If she gets really upset and seems like she needs you, then I'll have them stop the interview, and I'll come get you."

"We could do that?"

"I don't see why not."

Stan agreed to it without a second thought, and Mrs. Danes was visibly relieved. I might've felt the same way if I were hearing it from my own child.

Chloe did a great job. I was so proud of her. There were parts of her statement that would haunt me for years: when she described the way they held her face down in the pillow, and how she had to walk three miles home from the party bleeding. But as brutal as it'd been to hear, it didn't compare to what she'd been through, and I could handle being there for her statement as long as it brought her justice.

"Is there anything else? Anything else you can think of that might help us find the boys who did this to you?" Detective Wallace asked. Stan was there, too, along with the victim's advocate assigned to Chloe.

Chloe's eyes were red and puffy. She wore the same hoodie she'd had on when we first met, like a security blanket wrapped around her. We'd already taken two breaks when she'd broken down uncontrollably. Mrs. Danes came in to soothe her and left once Chloe felt ready to start again. It was a grueling process, but she was almost through it. She had to be exhausted. I hoped they'd let her take a nap after this.

"Anything at all." Stan's voice joined his partner's. "A smell? Like, maybe one of them had a distinct cologne or body odor?"

She shook her head. "I just remember the laughing. I hear their laughs on a loop in my head." It's the one thing she said over and over again. That part of the experience was cemented inside her.

Detective Wallace had explained earlier that our senses were remarkably accurate and helpful in identifying people. Especially with trauma victims, because trauma heightened our senses so much. Sometimes one compensated for the loss of another, so it made sense that Chloe would remember a sound so vividly when her sight was blocked out. If we could bring in every high school boy at Buckley and ask them to laugh, we'd probably find her attackers. But we couldn't do that.

She casually shrugged. "There is one more thing. But it's kind of embarrassing . . ."

"Don't be embarrassed, Chloe," I reassured her. "You're the victim of a crime, the survivor of an attack. Be proud of yourself for coming forward."

"Well . . . I think . . . I think . . ." Her cheeks flushed with humiliation and shame. She took a deep breath. "I think one of them might have taken my underwear."

Detective Wallace sat straight up in his chair the moment she said it. He couldn't hide his how-could-you-forget-something-that-important look as he stared at her. Stan wore the same dazed expression. But I don't think she'd been hiding this. I think she hadn't remembered until now. It was another marker of trauma, her mind wiping the memory from her until she was ready for it. The same thing happened to me—I remembered details of my attack months after the police interview. Trauma memories played by their own rules. You couldn't force them to appear or tell them what to do.

Or maybe it was because she was so young, and teenagers were always forgetting things. Either way, I knew Chloe by now—it wasn't intentional.

"Tell me more about it," Detective Wallace pressed, working hard to keep himself from rapid-firing questions at her. I could see it in the way he worked his jaw. How he was at the edge of his seat like it was difficult to stay put.

Chloe cringed and shrank into herself. I put my hand gently on her back. Gave her hand a gentle squeeze. "I just remember lying on my stomach with my head smashed in the pillow. I could barely breathe. Looking to the side with just one eye. And then . . . then, my underwear. My underwear was there on the pillow. Just sitting there next to me. I remember thinking, *How'd it get up there? What's my underwear doing on the pillow?* It was the moment I knew something was really wrong." She pulled her hand out from mine and twisted her hands together anxiously on her lap. "And then all the blurry stuff, you know? Like before? How I was telling you? It was like that. But I think somebody grabbed it. They put it around their wrist like a bracelet."

Stan nodded. His face went back to the blank slate he'd managed to wear most of the interview. "What did the underwear look like? Can you describe them for us?"

She turned bright red and looked at the floor. "So embarrassing . . . they were . . ." She cleared her throat. "They were white and said 'Yummy.' Oh, and they had an ice cream cone in the front . . ."

The information throttled me. The air was gone from my lungs immediately. My body was revolting against the violent memory forcing its way to the surface. Every muscle straining to move, to jump up from my chair and run as fast as I could, so the memory wouldn't catch me. But it did.

The underwear I'd found in Hunter's closet on the day I went searching. I remember they were white, and had writing on them. Did it say "Yummy"? I'd scrunched them into a ball and tossed them into his hamper as quickly as I could, but I could've sworn there was writing. Maybe I was wrong. I desperately wanted to be wrong. The room spun. Hit me like vertigo. I had to get out of there. I couldn't breathe. My heart was pounding. Not just in my chest, but in my ears, a violent whooshing sound.

Somehow, the interview ended, but I missed everything after that point—I had no idea what Chloe said or what happened next. I must've said goodbye and walked out of the hospital, but I didn't know how. I didn't remember the drive home, but everything came crystal clear—instantly sharp—when I stumbled into my house. I raced into the laundry room in the basement.

Laundry was my least favorite chore, same as Hunter. We both ignored it for as long as we could. Just stacked our clothes in baskets until we had no other choice but to do it. I'd started a load of my whites last night, so I'd sorted all my stuff, but Hunter's hamper stood there still filled with all the dirty clothes I'd brought down from his closet over a week ago. I dumped it out, frantically pawing my way through crusty socks, dirty uniforms, and smelly T-shirts. I couldn't find the underwear. But it had been there. Where was it? And then suddenly, I felt something. Like a ball of rolled-up socks in my hand. Pink, purple, and yellow strings tied into a knot, a handful of different women's underwear.

I untied them slowly.

One. Two. Three. Four.

They could all be his ex-girlfriends'. They could. None of them looked like Chloe's . . . and then, in the next breath—there they were. Tiny, white with "Yummy" scrawled in pink cursive coupled with a cute ice cream cone. Nausea filled my throat. I threw them like they'd burned me. Like they were the thing responsible. I sank to the floor.

This couldn't be happening.

Except that it was.

CHAPTER SEVENTEEN

"Hey, Mom," Hunter called. I heard his footsteps through the living room, like he was going upstairs up to his room like he usually did when he came home from school.

"Come into the dining room. I want to talk to you," I said. My pulse was pounding so hard it made my head hurt.

"Make it quick, because I've got a math test tomorrow and a bunch of other homework I've got to get done before I can even study." He popped into the room. His backpack was strapped to him. AirPods snug in his ears.

"I'm not messing around with you anymore," I said with my eyes locked on his, like a dog trying to establish dominance. I did my best to keep my voice steady. "You're going to tell me exactly what happened with Chloe at the party."

"Oh my god, Mom! Again?" He stomped and rolled his eyes. "Can we seriously be done with this? I told you. I'm over it!"

I flung the underwear on the table. "Well, I'm not. Want to tell me where these came from?"

He grimaced and backed away like he was scared to touch them. He put his hands up. "What the hell is this? Something is *really* wrong with you. Why are you throwing dirty underwear on the table? Where'd you get that?"

"Where did *you* get them, Hunter?" I yelled. I didn't mean to raise my voice, but I couldn't help it.

"Bruh, settle down." He looked even more annoyed. "Probably from the last girl I pulled."

I jumped up from my chair and leapt in front of him, unable to control myself anymore. "This is Chloe's underwear!" I grabbed it from the table and shook it at him, flailing it in his face. "Now you tell me what happened. This is your last chance!"

"God, Mom. That's *not* Chloe's underwear. Those are Raven's, I recognize them now." He tried to snatch them away, but I wouldn't let him. This was the only physical evidence we had. "I don't know what's up with you and that girl, but you need to chill. I'm starting to actually get mad now."

"Oh, *you're* starting to get mad?" I stabbed my finger into his chest. "If you don't start telling the truth, you'll have a lot more to be mad about. These are the exact same underwear that Chloe said she was wearing the night of the attack. She described everything about them—the color, the design, the writing. And guess where I found them? In your closet."

"So what?" He took a step back. "Do you know how many girls have that exact same pair of underwear? They all shop at the same places. You need to get over it." He turned around and stormed out of the room, stomping up the stairs like he used to do when he was a toddler throwing a tantrum. "And you might want to think about getting some help. This is turning into a weird obsession," he yelled right before slamming his bedroom door.

I stood there next to the table holding the dirty underwear in my hand. I'd never considered the possibility they were someone else's. But Hunter was right—all the teenagers shopped at the same places. We only had one mall in town. Was he right that my obsession was clouding my judgment? Was I just being paranoid?

If James wasn't his father, would I still be afraid that he could be capable of this? I tried to steady my thoughts, but they were all over the place.

There was only one way to know if they were hers. I stepped outside and called Stan. He didn't answer, but called back within seconds.

"What's up?" His voice was hurried. I couldn't imagine how much pressure he was under. Nothing like this had ever happened in this town, and now everybody knew.

I struggled not to cry. I wasn't supposed to be doing this. Mothers protected their children at all costs. But what if your child was the one others needed protecting from? *Please don't let it be true.* I clutched the dirty underwear in my hand.

"Stan, you know how Chloe described the underwear she was wearing and how one of the boys took them? Well . . ." For a second, I felt as though I stepped outside of myself, watching myself from a safe distance, as I laid out my suspicions about my own son. It felt unnatural. All of it, horribly wrong. "The truth is, things haven't felt right about Hunter since this happened. He was at the party that night and was supposed to be staying overnight at a friend's house afterward, but he called me in the middle of the night to come pick him up. When he got in the car, there was a scratch on his neck and a mark on his cheek. I tried to figure it all out myself—I really did. Even if he was involved, I wanted to know the truth. I asked him about the fight, the party, the video. Chloe. Multiple times. I even searched his room." I could feel myself getting sidetracked by my feelings. I had to stay focused. "When I cleaned his closet last week, I found women's underwear. I figured they were his ex-girlfriend's, because some of her other stuff was there, too. I hadn't thought about any of it until today. Not until we were sitting with Chloe and she described the underwear. That's when I remembered. I found underwear in Hunter's closet, and I think it's hers. It's . . . it's the exact pair she described."

He was silent, digesting everything I'd just said. The space stretched out between us. He didn't try to hide the disapproval in his voice when he spoke again. "It would've been helpful to have this information about Hunter when we started the investigation. I'm not happy you kept it a secret."

"I know, and I didn't intentionally keep it from you, but—" I cut off midsentence. The truth was that I did. I started over. "I didn't know what to do, Stan. He's my son. And I honestly couldn't tell if Hunter's stuff was related or just a bunch of coincidences. All I wanted to do was save Chloe. Just help her. That's all. I didn't want Hunter's mess getting in the way. I never believed he was actually involved and never . . . I'm sorry if it took me awhile, but I'm his mother, and I didn't want it to be true. You can't blame me for that." And he couldn't. This was a parent's worst nightmare, and he was a parent, too. I swallowed hard. I didn't even know how to say it. Once the words were out of my mouth, I couldn't take them back. The magnitude of the situation washed over me. "I kept hoping things would play out differently, and it wasn't until halfway through the investigation that I even started suspecting him. Here's the deal, Stan. All I had before were suspicions. That was it. The moment I found any real evidence indicating that he might have anything to do with Chloe's attack, I brought it to you. He's barely gone upstairs from our conversation."

"You really think he might have something to do with this?" Stan had met Hunter a few times over the years and we bumped into each other quite frequently at various functions. I spent the first five minutes of every conversation gushing about whatever was going on in his life, so on some level, Stan had grown up with him. And even though he was mad about me keeping my suspicions from him, the way he asked was telling me I better be sure. That I needed to think carefully about opening this door, because once we did, there'd be no shutting it. We would live in a different world.

I knew that no matter how the investigation ultimately resolved, Hunter would forever be guilty in a town this small. That was just how it worked. If they suspected you of something, you were as good as done. Hunter's entire future would be ruined by this. There'd be no going back. It was my last chance to get out, but I didn't take it. Instead, I did what was right. What I should've done a long time ago.

"Yes, I think there's a possibility Hunter assaulted Chloe."

CHAPTER EIGHTEEN

I waited anxiously in the visitors' lounge at the jail. Standing up, sitting down, standing again. Walking back and forth across the narrow space. The DNA test took ninety minutes to run. Stan had stayed with me on the phone all the way down here and walked me through the front door, talking me through everything that was about to happen step by step. He told me to go home, and that he'd call me when they had results. That it might actually be longer than ninety minutes, because they were really backed up. But I couldn't bring myself to go home.

What if Hunter came downstairs while I was there? What would I say to him? What would I do? There was no way I could act normal and keep this all a secret. It was better to stay and wait, not to approach him again until I knew for sure.

It'd been ninety-seven excruciatingly long minutes since they put the underwear in a plastic bag and carried them to the back. That wasn't the only thing I gave them: I grabbed Hunter's toothbrush from his bathroom before I left the house, too. I even pulled a couple of hairs from the sink and put them in a Ziploc baggie just in case, but they hadn't needed them—the toothbrush worked just fine.

I didn't tell Hunter where I was going or what I was doing, just texted to say I was running an errand. Nothing from him since.

Stan came through the door wearing a grim expression and I knew the results without him needing to say a word. He announced it like a doctor delivering a terminal diagnosis—straightforward, honest, and to the point. "The DNA on the underwear matched Chloe's. There was also DNA from three males, and yes, one of the samples matches Hunter's." I felt the color draining from my face, and he wasn't done talking. There was more.

I'd brought the other pairs of women's underwear along with Chloe's and turned them in with hers. I didn't even know why, really, I'd just done it. They'd taken samples and run the DNA on each. "His DNA is on all the other underwear, too. We're running those samples through our databases, and that's going to take a significant amount of time. However, we already have a match on one of the pairs." My mind raced. Why would the girls Hunter hooked up with be in the police databases? They were high school girls— sweet, innocent kids I'd fed dinners and asked about college plans.

Stan steeled himself. He didn't want to tell me, but he had to. "It's a rape case from two months ago. Remember how I mentioned there were a couple of other open investigations?"

My hand flew to my mouth.

Stan's face shifted from detective to friend as soon as he'd delivered the news. "I'm so sorry, Felicia. I'm just as shocked as you are. They're connected to those cases." He reached out like he wanted to hug me. "Do you want to sit down?"

I didn't want to sit down. I wanted to jump out of my skin. Scream at the top of my lungs. How could this be happening? I was a good parent. Good parents didn't raise criminals. That's not how it worked. What did this mean? Who *was* my son? I still loved him. I loved him so much. What could I do now?

I stumbled back into the chair. I felt the fake leather padded seat. The one I'd gotten up and down from while I waited to see which way my world would spin. I'd hoped and prayed. But deep down, I knew. A mother always knows.

"What do we do now?" I asked. My body had gone from being unable to sit still to frozen. And tired, all of a sudden—a wave of exhaustion pummeled me.

"We're going to charge him with first-degree sexual assault. The DA wants to come out hard with this one, to set a precedent from the very beginning." He looked sorry to tell me.

"So . . . what now? We just go to my house, and you put him in handcuffs?" The entire neighborhood would see. Everyone would talk. They were going to dissect our lives, pick us apart piece by piece until we weren't even real people anymore. And what would they find when they looked at me? Where had I gone wrong? What had I done?

"I know—I don't want to cause a scene, either. I trust you. If you want, you can go home and get him, then bring him back here to turn himself in."

Stan could trust me, but I couldn't trust Hunter. Not anymore. The truth was that if I went home, I wasn't sure he'd come back to the police station with me. What if he stuck to his story and refused? He'd shown no remorse so far. And I couldn't physically make him get in the car. He was bigger and stronger than me now. Would he get angry? What would I do then? Would he hurt me? I didn't know. It was a devastating blow. Our world was never going to be the same, because I was afraid of my son in a way no mother ever should be.

"Thank you, Stan, but I'm not sure he'll go with me. You might have to come with," I said. Everything felt like a dream. So many of my clients talked about this when they'd been blindsided by their partners' leaving: that it didn't feel real. That they felt like they were living in an alternate universe. I'd never really understood it until now, but I'd never felt so removed from my body. Like one giant head floating around; unattached. "I know you're busy, but . . . do you think you can?"

"Sure, of course," Stan said, doing a quick pat down of his pockets to make sure he had everything on him that he needed. I'd never been so grateful for his friendship as I followed him out the station door.

Hunter had lied to me. Straight to my face. Over and over again. Even when he was confronted with real evidence, he'd clung to his claims of innocence. Something about that scared me almost as much as what he'd done. How could he behave this way?

"Do you want me to drive?" Stan asked when we got to my car, and I tossed him the keys because I definitely couldn't handle it. My thoughts were jumping all over the place. My nerves were firecrackers popping off inside my body. I'd never known anxiety like this. The kind that made you want to go straight to the emergency room and tell them you were having a heart attack.

"Breathe, Felicia. Breathe," I said it out loud because saying it silently wasn't working.

Stan put his hand on my back and gently guided me into the passenger seat. "It's going to be okay."

But it wasn't.

Because my son was a rapist.

Please no. I thought. *Not my son.*

And then it struck me, like I'd been jolted with electricity. It was always somebody's son.

We assumed parents were as bad as their kids. Hunter wouldn't be the only one considered guilty of his crimes. I would be judged just as harshly. It didn't matter how open-minded and empathetic we pretended to be with other parents. When kids were fucked up, we pointed the finger directly at the parents, especially the mothers.

I'd done the same thing my whole life. It never occurred to me that a kid could do something terrible if they had a nurturing home, with good parents who instilled good values. Not that I was perfect. I certainly wasn't. I was way too permissive. I remembered spoiling him with toys when he was little because I felt guilty over him not having a father or siblings. I cried way too much in front of him, and I'd snapped at him more than once when I was exhausted by the challenges of single parenthood. But for the most part our home had been kind, loving, and stable. That was the most important thing to me once I decided to have him.

Except that didn't matter. He'd still turned out bad. Not cheating on a test or shoplifting bad. This was vile. I always thought of myself as a good mom. Being Hunter's mom was as natural to me as breathing. It was the thing I was best at. And now he'd turned bad. Or he'd always been bad. I didn't know. Nothing made sense anymore.

I didn't notice I was crying until I wiped the tears on the back of my sleeve. I rolled down the window, sticking my head out like a dog. There wasn't enough air. "I don't think I can do this."

"It'll be okay. You'll get through this," Stan assured me, just like I'd assured Chloe. I thought back to that first conversation, which felt like a lifetime ago. Telling her that everything would be okay. I didn't believe him any more than she'd believed me.

What would happen to Hunter? Would I have to pay for his trial? His lawyers? I didn't want to. I didn't want to do any of that. He was dangerous, and if he was found guilty, he deserved to go to jail.

Would I keep him in my house? Even if he did serve time, what would I do when he got out? Would he turn on me, angry for turning him in? What kind of violence was he capable of? How far would he go? My thoughts chased themselves in circles.

"You're going to get through this," Stan said again, because what else could he say? I didn't have a choice to stop being

Hunter's mom. Even though I wanted to. In that moment, I'd never wanted anything more.

Within minutes, we were back at my house, but I couldn't get out of the car. Stan came around and opened the door for me. He held out his arm. I shook my head, but I had to get up. We both knew that. My legs were lead as he escorted me down the sidewalk and toward the house. Would Hunter run if he saw me with Stan? I couldn't predict any of his behavior. I didn't even know him anymore. Had I ever? That was the saddest part. I almost crumpled on the sidewalk.

"I've got you," Stan said. One hand on my elbow. The other on my back.

I turned to look at him right before we stepped inside. "What happens if he doesn't go?"

"Then I arrest him."

I gulped and we moved into the house without another word. It was quiet inside, but Hunter's backpack and shoes were at the door. He was definitely home.

"Hunter?" I called out. My voice weak and wavery. He'd know from the sound of it that something was wrong. "Can you come downstairs for a sec?"

His footsteps thundered above us and then he appeared at the top of the stairs. He froze when he saw me standing in the entryway with Stan. I couldn't speak.

"Hey, Hunter," Stan said like he'd just stopped by to visit after work, like it was any other day. "I don't know if you've noticed, but we've been at the school talking with some of your classmates and friends about the assault on Chloe Danes. We haven't had a chance to talk to you about the incident, so I'd like it if you'd come down to the station with me and your mom to answer some questions."

Hunter crossed his arms on his chest defiantly and stared down at us with a huge scowl on his face. "I already told my mom—I don't remember anything about that night."

"It's protocol, since you were at the party. We're interviewing everyone who was there that night. We can talk about all that down at the station," Stan said, maintaining a neutral tone and stance.

Hunter shook his head. "I'm not going to the police station with you." He shook it again. "No, I'm not going down there. I already told you what I know."

"Hunter, you don't have a choice," I said, finally finding my voice.

He glared at me, and turned around like he was going to head back to his room. Stan dashed up the stairs before he could get far and grabbed his arm. He whipped him around.

"You're coming with me." Stan's tone wasn't neutral this time. He meant business. I'd never heard him sound more like a police officer than in that moment.

Suddenly, Hunter realized what was happening, and his eyes searched mine for understanding. Waiting for me to make it better. To do something to help him, because that's what I did. That was my job. I was his mother.

I spoke quietly, my voice almost a whisper. "I took all the underwear I found in your closet to the police, and they ran the DNA."

His mouth hung open as he read the betrayal stamped all over my face. He knew exactly what I had done. What it meant. He slowly closed his mouth. His eyes narrowed to slits. A darkness clouded his features.

And in that moment, something inside of him died. Right in front of my eyes. It was as if Stan had showed up at my door and told me there'd been a terrible accident, and my son hadn't survived. The person I thought I knew, who I loved so fiercely, was gone.

The only thing left to do was cry.

EPILOGUE

Six months later

I stood in the living room surveying the boxes stacked against the walls. All of them sealed with tape and labeled with black marker by what was inside. The movers would be here in twenty minutes. I'd been so nervous working up to this day. How would I feel when I left the home I raised my son in?

I couldn't help picturing all that had once been here. The hallway leading from the living room into the family room that proudly displayed Hunter's artwork and achievements. I started doing it in preschool and never stopped. I thought about the office on the other end of the second floor that had gone through three rounds of remodeling as the house aged right along with us. First an office, then a baby's room, and back to an office after he'd moved down the hallway into the bedroom across from me. The walls in the family room that we'd painted together. Twice. The fireplace where we'd hung our stockings every Christmas. Hunter leaving milk and cookies out for Santa, no matter how old he was. The refrigerator covered in pictures. Old school photos we still printed out and hung with magnets.

But all that was gone.

Now the walls stood barren. Stripped down to nothing. The only signs of life left in the house were the dirty fingerprints on the walls and the indentations from our furniture on the carpet. All the remnants of us and who we were, carefully sealed away in boxes. Ones I wasn't sure I'd ever open again. It was like burying a relative. Some people kept their homes as shrines to their loved ones, but they didn't have a child like mine. Since the moment he'd been born, I'd walked through life like there was an invisible umbilical cord still connecting us. Like even though they'd cut the cord, we were still together. That connection was gone now. Completely severed. I couldn't even feel him anymore.

At first, I'd wrapped myself in a warm blanket of denial while he sat in jail awaiting trial. There were moments of reprieve. Times when I convinced myself that he was on drugs so he didn't know what he was doing; that the underwear had been planted in his room by one of his friends; or that he'd somehow been co-erced into doing what he did. That was the theory I fell on most often—that there was someone who forced him to do these hor-rible things and he didn't have any other choice.

That was until I read the police report and saw the video. Stan forced me to do it. He said I needed to know the whole truth. The report described how he'd stalked the girls on social media first. Learning everything he could about their lives before he ever ap-proached them with a fake account. He had all kinds of aliases and backstories. Shifting and dissolving who he was, depending on the person he was talking to.

It hadn't been hard to figure out what he'd done and what he was planning after they arrested him and got search warrants for all of his things. Their search of his room was as futile as mine had been, but they found all sorts of stuff I'd missed when they went through his phone. They even found another phone I knew nothing about. Purchased and paid for with a credit card I was just as oblivious to. The phone led them to a storage locker he'd been renting for cheap on the other side of town for almost a year. He used it as a makeshift office. From there, it was easy to discover everything he'd done because he kept a journal. It was meticulous and thorough, as if all of it was a well-researched science project for school.

Turns out, Hunter had never intended to share the video. One of the other boys involved in the assault asked for it and threatened to tell what he'd done to Chloe if Hunter didn't give him a copy. He'd been the one to share it with everyone. The video was worse than I'd even imagined. It was just like Stan said—cruel, mocking laughter toward a girl they'd just brutalized. I understood the reason it was seared into Chloe's consciousness the way it was. I'd never work it out of my system either. Hunter had recorded Chloe like he'd recorded all the others on his secret phone. And the thing no one had been able to recognize that I did? Hunter was the one doing most of the laughing. The others in the room were only following his lead. Sinister. Cold. Cruel and mocking. That's how he sounded. That's who he was on the inside. Rotten.

And he was only getting started. His writings included detailed plans of what he intended to do next. They included torture, and he even toyed with the idea of what it would feel like to end the life of another human being. That's the thing he wrote about the most. The thought that brought him the most excitement. Even his handwriting changed when he described the things he wanted to do to innocent girls. I had to take breaks while I was reading it, like Chloe had to take breaks in her interview.

I was gutted.

Despite all the evidence, I don't think he ever would've gotten caught if I hadn't found the underwear. They were the only things he brought from the storage locker into the house—I guess he couldn't help himself. He needed to see his trophies. Keep them close. Who knows how long this would've continued to go undetected if I hadn't had a reason to look. Thinking he was smarter than everyone else around him wasn't just a delusion of grandeur either—he was highly intelligent. Forensic psychologists performed all kinds of psychological tests and evaluations while he awaited trial. His IQ was 162—a certifiable genius. Exceptionally gifted. Most sociopaths were. That was the other thing they'd diagnosed him with: antisocial personality disorder with psychopathic features.

He'd played me. And who could say when it all started. There were so many theories on sociopathy, and I'd devoured them all. But I always come back to the first feature listed in the diagnostic criteria in the *DSM-5*: *A pervasive pattern of disregard for and violation of the rights of others present by age 15.* That's who he was. My son didn't care about other people.

I clung to groups on Facebook with parents whose kids had done terrible things, because except for a few people like Elaine and my best friend, no one in Eagle Rock wanted to come anywhere near me. Not just because of what Hunter had done, but because of the utter fear it struck in people about the possibility I might be telling the truth—that I had been a good parent.

And I had been. What did that mean for all of them?

I gave Hunter everything. And not just the material things. I provided way more than a roof over his head and all the basic necessities. I showered him with the things that were the most important—love, truth, empathy, compassion. Being a good human being. That's the thing that was always most important to me.

But nobody wanted to hear that. Nobody wanted to believe a bad kid could be raised by a good parent. That your child could be a sociopath and you would have no clue you were living with one under your roof. Buying them clothes and feeding them breakfast. Taking them to the mall. That was too terrifying.

So, instead, they said other things about me. Created alternate explanations. Ones that made them feel safe. Fit in their box. They painted me as a neglectful parent more focused on my career than on my child. They talked about how many cases I'd tried last year and as supporting evidence the awards I'd won. My skin was thick enough to survive the gossip, but I refused to live with the death threats that started coming as soon as the story broke. Chloe had already left town by then. Mr. and Mrs. Danes had put their house on the market while she was still in the hospital, and they'd moved back east to live near Mrs. Danes's family. They knew Chloe would never be able to get a fresh start if she stayed and probably never feel safe either. And she seemed to be making friends and adjusting well at her new school, according to the occasional texts she'd send me—this time, from her real number.

Stan would be here any minute to help me pack up a U-Haul and move on to my own fresh start. He was the only good thing that'd come out of all of this and I was glad my new place was only a few hours away so we could keep seeing each other. He hadn't left my side since the day he arrested Hunter. There was no way I could've navigated my way through this without him. I wouldn't say I loved him yet, but I liked him a whole lot and I loved having him around. It was just like when my sister died—after the initial trauma and shock, everyone just wants you to hurry up and feel better. Nobody likes living in darkness. But Stan was different. He lived in it every day, so what I was going through didn't bother him the way it did other people. I was so grateful to have him.

Hunter still called from jail every few days. I used to take his calls out of guilt and obligation. After all, you couldn't just stop being someone's mother. Or so I thought. But he would call enraged, absolutely furious at me because I refused to defend him or send him any money. So I'd hang up, and he'd call back a sweet, kind child, as if he hadn't just cussed me out and told me he hoped the house burned down with me inside it. It wasn't long before I stopped taking his calls. Turns out, a mother's love isn't unconditional after all. At least not mine.

Stan honked from outside to let me know he was here. The movers were probably outside, too, by now. I let out a long deep sigh, then took one last look, and closed the door behind me.

ACKNOWLEDGMENTS

One of Our Own was one of my most enjoyable writing projects this year because it was so unique. First, so grateful for partnering with Simon & Schuster Audio on this work. I couldn't have created this story without the keen editorial eye of Lara Blackman. For the amazing narrators: A. J. Cook and Tessa Albertson. Thank you. They brought these characters to life in an incredible way. To all my readers: you're my most favorite part. Thank you for always supporting me.

Made in the USA
Middletown, DE
19 January 2026

27302029R00081